NEW KID IN TOWN

by
Janette Oke

NEW KID IN TOWN

by

Janette Oke

Illustrated by Brenda Mann

All author's rights and royalties
on this book
have been assigned to
COMPASSION INTERNATIONAL
a non-profit organization
dedicated to helping
needy children
around the world.

ISBN 0-934998-16-7

Printed in U.S.A.

Dedicated
to Mary Frank teacher
and my 'special'
life-long friend

ELEANOR QUANTZ

During the school year of 1981-1982, I visited a grade five English class at Mary Frank Elementary School and found them to be especially excited about all forms of writing and the procedure from plotting and research to publication. I enjoyed sharing with this group and when their teacher, Eleanor Quantz, urged me to write a story about a skunk, I decided to let the children become involved as well. They did research about the living habits of skunks, wrote out suggestions for names (which I have used in many instances), made a list of ideas for the story 'happenings' (which in most cases I did not use—they were primarily exciting space adventures or 'skunk deliverance' from the Russians), and submitted to me a number of forest friends that could be included in the story.

To these students I say "thank you." I hope that you enjoy seeing our book in print. I know that you will agree that it takes many months before an author gets from an idea to a book on the bookstore shelves.

My sincere best wishes for success in your future, whatever you decide to do in life. Maybe someday I will be reading and enjoying your book.

Janette

Edward Ludwig
Sheryl Salo
Chris Barouska
Gregg Greene
Wendy Stokman
Linda Freeland
Danny Coffman
Dana Fodrocy
Jimmy Nevelle
Mike Crawford
Tracy Matthews
David Anderson
Jeff Minix
Kim Weston
Christina Minix
Muir Daffron
Ann Paul
Eric Macht
David Gardner
Bobby Higgins
Jim Griffin
Scott Laudeman
Bart Cole
Michele Brown
Debbie Wittle

Steve Lemme
Mike Bockman
Andy Tomasik
Elizabeth Dannaway
Justine Snyder
Brian Goodman
Dana Peterson

Chapter One

The midsummer moon hung in the cloud-scattered sky like a free-floating pale yellow bubble. I glanced at it, but even the usual fascination that I felt in watching it bob in and out of the fleecy cloud cover failed to hold my attention. There were far too many other things for me to see and feel on this delightful night. Things that I had never seen or heard or felt before. I breathed deeply and then stopped for a quick sniff, thrusting my nose into the soft freshness of ground under a log that lay slowly rotting near the path that I had been ordered to follow. The odors that I encountered there excited me and I hesitated for a better whiff.

"Fuzzle!"

Mother's sharp voice brought my attention back to what I was supposed to be doing. Mother heartily disapproved of disobedience, and lagging behind the rest of the family was high on her list of forbidden behavior. I jerked back my inquisitive nose and trotted on down the trail.

This was our training period. We were the students—

all six of us—and Mother was the teacher, and a good one she was, too. Already we had been taught to sniff carefully before leaving the den, to walk in single file, to move forward slowly in all circumstances, and to listen to Mother at all times. She decided when it was time to leave the den for the evening dinner hour, she showed us what was proper food for us to dine upon, she led us to the best water supply, she knew when to hold her ground and when to surrender the path when meeting other creatures of the woodland. She also decided when it was time for us to return to our beds, and once we were on the way home she did not like dallying. I was dallying, and her reproach strongly suggested that I fall back in order at the end of the home-going line. I did. At least for awhile I did. But with Sparkey, Odar, Pokey, Phew, and little Schatze all between Mother and me, it was very easy for my attention to wander and for me to forget that I was supposed to be marching smartly along. I tried. I really did. But there were so many interesting things for me to see and smell that it was very hard for me to pass them all by. So I trotted along at the end of the line, allowing myself a brief excursion here and a slight diversion there. Little by little Mother and the rest of the family were lengthening the distance between them and me. I couldn't imagine how they could be in such a hurry to return home. All that awaited us there was a day of sleeping.

I hurried my footsteps some in an effort to catch up and tried to keep my mind on following my family. It would have worked too if I hadn't spotted some strange looking contraptions stacked nearby at the edge of Mr. Willougby's grocery store lot. There was a delightful smell coming from them. I decided to get a closer look and that's when my troubles really began.

It was a new and strange odor that greeted me, but it smelled so good it made my tummy tickle. Whatever it was that promised to be so tasty was locked away in the confines of the crates.

I crawled up on one of them and pushed my nose under the lid, forcing my head in so that I could get a better look. As I pushed hard against the resisting lid, I lost my footing and fell, "plop," down upon the hard slats of the crate bottom. At first I was foolish enough to be pleased with myself. I was near the good smell and I hurriedly busied myself nosing along the slats and licking up every morsel of left-behind goodies. I didn't know just what it was that I was eating. Mother had never identified it for me, but it was very tasty. As I neared the end of it I felt keenly disappointed that there was no more, though I'm sure that my already-full tummy couldn't have held another bite. When I was convinced that it truly was all gone, I decided to hurry on after Mother and the family. Perhaps if I hustled she wouldn't have noticed that I was missing.

As I nosed my way around the crate looking for its doorway, I found that it had none—at least not where I could reach it. The only opening that I could see at all was way above my head. As I looked up and up, I could see the slight opening where I had pushed my way through to gain entrance. Beyond that small crack the stars were still twinkling, but their lights were already beginning to get dim and I knew that the night would soon be giving way to the day. Mother always liked to have us safely tucked away in our den before the day creatures began to prowl. She would be looking for me, angry that I had fallen out of line. I felt for a moment that I was glad that I was hidden from her and I pressed myself into the darkest corner, expecting at any time for her to poke her nose through the opening above me and scold me sharply for my carelessness.

As time ticked slowly by, I forgot to be concerned about

Mother's anger and became concerned instead that she wouldn't be able to find me. I pushed myself as near to the opening above my head as I could and even tried to jump the impossible distance a few times. It didn't work. There was no way that I could jump high enough. Still, I didn't want to give up. I jumped and clawed at the side of the box until I was exhausted. Finally, tired and discouraged, I gave up and curled up in a corner. I would just have to wait for Mother. The awkward slats of the crate dug into my full sides, but in spite of my discomfort, I did manage to go to sleep, hoping that it would not be too long until Mother would come back looking for me.

I was awakened by a lot of noise. The sun was up, shining down heartily on the world. It was the time for sleeping—not stirring—but all around me were loud, bustling beings who did not seem to be smart enough to know that. They were banging and clanging their way through the crates.

For a moment fear gripped me. What would happen when they reached mine? And then a small hope took hold of me. Why, they'd set me free of course, and then I would be able to hurry home to Mother. I hoped that I would be able to find my way in the bright sunshine.

I waited excitedly for them to reach my crate, but when they did, I was not even noticed and my crate was lifted and stacked with the rest.

After what seemed like an awfully long time the two noisy humans slammed some doors, and the place where the crates were now resting began to shiver and shake as a great roaring sound started right beneath me. Then I began to move, slowly at first, and then faster and faster, the wind whizzing and whining through the cracks of the crates. On and on I went. I tried to sleep but it was useless. The noise and the rattling kept me awake. I began to wonder if those humans were ever going to reach their den. At times it was very hot and I was thankful for the cool wind that whipped around me. I was thirsty and tired, and my once-full tummy was not as contented anymore.

Finally the roaring stopped and the humans began to lift the crates again. I was so glad to be back. Now I could get on with the business of letting Mother know where I was.

One after the other the crates were slammed and banged into position. The humans were lifting them all from the noisy, moving machine onto a platform. At last they came to mine, and again I hoped that they might notice me. They didn't. They stacked my crate with the others, slammed doors, started the roaring sound again, and were gone.

After the noise had all gone away, I pressed myself to the side of the crate and looked out at the world. To my amazement I discovered that I wasn't back where I had started from at all. In fact I had never in my life seen the place on which the crates were now stacked. How far was I from Mother and the den anyway? Would it be a long walk? Would I be able to smell my way home? I went back to a corner and curled up as tightly as I could. I was forced to face my problem squarely. Here I was—aching, thirsty, frightened, and perhaps a long way from home. The hard crate held me prisoner. It was not even comfortable and it offered no more food than what I had already pilfered the night before. Evening was coming and, though I welcomed the coolness, I was beginning to get awfully hungry. My instincts told me that it was the time of day when I should be starting out to find something to eat—but how could I?

How I wished that I had listened to Mother. She had

tried so many times to warn me that my inquisitiveness could get me into a lot of trouble. I had now learned my lesson, but would I ever find my way out?

I looked over my head at the lid, still in position though not fastened securely. Through the boards I could see the blue evening sky with white fluffy clouds drifting carelessly overhead. I thought of the games that I had played with my brothers and sisters of finding objects in the cloud formations.

"See there," one of us would shout, "it looks like a great big, giant caterpillar."

"Over there," would squeal someone else, "see—it's a frog."

"And that one—see it—right up there. It's a grasshopper."

"Where? Where?"

"Right there."

"I see it! I see it!"

Thinking of the game now only made me feel hungrier. I tried to curl up more tightly so that my complaining stomach wouldn't hurt as much, but it didn't seem to help.

Finally, I just gave up and let big tears run down my furry cheeks, falling *splash* on the narrow slats beneath me. Whatever would happen to me now?

Chapter Two

I slept fitfully, off and on, even though my own instincts told me clearly that this was not "sleeping time" but "eating time." However, there was nothing to eat, and in order to forget the agony of my empty stomach I tried hard to sleep.

Sometime during the night my napping was interrupted by a strange sound. Someone was sniffing around the crates. At first I had a wild hope that it might be Mother, but I knew that it wasn't Mother's smell that reached my sensitive nose. It was a strange smell. In fact, I didn't remember ever having encountered it before, at least not in the wilds. The sniffing still continued, "sniff, sniff, sniff," and it was getting closer and closer.

There was bumping and shoving of the crates as the animal made his way back and forth. It must be a large animal, I concluded, in order to push the crates around in such a manner.

Finally he came to my crate and his sniffing made him wildly excited. He made a funny "woofing" sound and began to scratch at the lid. Sore and achy though I was, I was on my feet immediately, for I wanted to welcome him when he made his appearance.

His sniffing increased and he began to push and shove even harder. The next thing I knew my crate was tumbling and banging end-over-end, and I was tumbling and banging end-over-end, too. It was a horrid experience. I wondered if I'd ever stop rolling and pitching—but at last I did.

I picked myself up and shook myself, testing to see if I had any broken bones. Everything seemed to still be in place so I gingerly took a step forward.

The crate now laid on its side, and the lid was askew from the beating that it had taken in the fall. To my surprise and joy, I noticed that there was room for one very small skunk to squeeze his way out. I moved forward to gladly do so and the sniffing started again.

I was glad that my rescuer was still around. I wanted to thank him. I wasn't sure how I would ever be able to voice my deep gratitude but I was anxious for the opportunity to try. I felt that I was willing to do almost anything for him in return for his rescue of me. I pushed my body through the small opening and squirmed my way out, then went to meet my deliverer who was still busily sniffing at the other side of the box.

I guess I expected him to greet me just as eagerly as I intended to greet him—but he didn't.

In fact he took one good look at me and his ears lifted right straight up and he backed up a pace. I still trotted, rather wobbly, toward him, anxious to express my thanks; but he didn't even wait to hear them. With one wild "yip" he turned and was gone like a streak, his tail tucked between his legs and his eyes looking wildly about.

I don't know why he acted like he did. You would have thought that I meant him harm or something. I wondered as I watched him race away if he had ever *met* a skunk before.

Chapter Three

The first order of business after being freed from the crate was to find something to satisfy the gnawing in my stomach. This had to be done even before I started my search for my way home. I was sure that I must have traveled a long way, and in order to be able to walk the long distance back I needed to have some proper nourishment.

Mother had really just begun our training program. Up until a few days prior to my misadventure, she had still been providing all of the nourishment that we needed; so I wasn't too sure just what all was considered edible for a properly-raised skunk. With my tummy growling and complaining, I decided that anything that I could chew would do. The problem seemed to be to find that *something.*

I set out, stiff and shaky. I sniffed the light breeze in the direction that I was headed, but no smell of food was in the air. I turned myself completely around, sniffing as I turned, but still no smell of food. I didn't know which direction I should head, so I just started out. Ahead I could see green things growing, tall trees and bushy shrubs. I hoped that it meant woodland creatures and food for a growing skunk and I coaxed my wobbly legs into a trot.

When I reached the edge of the forest, I plunged headlong into the underbrush, daring to hope that my noisy approach might scare up—not scare off—something for my dinner. I was disappointed. There was not a stir. I slowed to a walk, sniffing to each side of me as I padded on.

I smelled many things that were strange to me. Other animals lived nearby; I could tell by the scents. I wished that I could find one of them so that I could ask him where the food supply was. As alive and fresh as the scents were, I never did come upon them. Once or twice I even noticed the stirring of the bushes or grasses very nearby, but I never was able to spot anyone.

I walked on and on, deeper and deeper into the woods. I was about to give up, when I came upon a wild strawberry patch. It had been well picked by larger creatures than I, I guessed, by the way that the plants were trampled down. Whoever it was had left a few berries here and there, and I rushed around eagerly collecting them. A few of them had an ant or other insect to go along with the berries. It was a help, but scavenge as I did, it satisfied me very little. My poor tummy still grumbled even after I had gulped down every berry that I could find.

When I was convinced that I had eaten all of the berries in the patch, I moved on. I did find a cricket or two as I passed down the trail and a few grubs that lay unhidden after some larger animal had turned over a log.

I wandered on and on, my tired legs begging for a rest and my hungry stomach pleading to be fed. If only I could find something, even some water. Then I could fill my stomach with the liquid and perhaps convince it that the water was enough to meet its present needs.

I looked up at the sky. The moon had moved on to the west now; and, like me, it appeared tired and ready to go to bed. Soon the sun would be waking, stretching, and crawling out to waken birds and other daytime creatures. I needed to find a place where I could sleep. It was too late now to begin my search for Mother and the family. I would need to wait until the next time the moon climbed into the sky. I did wish that I could find a bit more to fill my empty stomach first.

I hastened onward, willing my legs to keep on moving. The moon slipped away below the western treeline and the golden rays of the sun began to streak the eastern sky, announcing that the sun itself would soon be making its daily appearance.

There was no water. There was no food. I badly needed rest and a place to hide away during the hours of the day.

I pushed my nose into the grasses, licking drops of dew in thirsty sips. It was inadequate, but it was something. I chewed a few blades of the grass. I couldn't remember Mother ever saying that grass was on our menu but it was something to put in my stomach. I made faces as I swallowed the distasteful stuff but forced down a few more bites. I didn't know how any animal could stand such a diet. It was most disagreeable. The dew that clung to the blades helped to make it at least bearable.

After I had eaten as much as I felt I could stand, I shook my head, choking down the last swallow, and decided to find a place to sleep. Oh, what I would have given for a tucked-away, cozy den. I had no idea where to look to find such a place. I wondered if one of the unseen animals that lived in the woodland would be willing to share his with me—just until I was able to find my own, of course. There was no one around to ask. I had never felt so lonely and deserted before. Why, I had always felt that the forest was the friendliest place one could ever be. Ours was always stirring with activity and business. True, Mother and the rest of us had pretty well kept to ourselves but we had been very aware of the other creatures. Now it seemed that I was totally alone. Not another creature seemed to be stirring, either in the grasses or the branches. I couldn't decide what was worse—the hunger that gnawed at my stomach or the loneliness that gnawed at my heart.

I began in earnest my search for a proper den, for the sun was telling me that I was past due in getting to bed. I found nothing. Mother hadn't yet taught us how to go about finding and preparing a home. I was about to give up when I found a rotten log that didn't appear to be inhabited. I crawled in. Now a den should be lined with soft grasses and mosses that would give the bed a comfortable feeling, only I wasn't sure how to go about that. Even if I had known, there was no time now to be out searching for suitable bedding material, so I just curled up toward the back of the opening and attempted to go to sleep. The hollow log was almost as uncomfortable as the crate of the night before. My bruised and aching bones and muscles protested against the hardness of my bed. The loneliness seeped all through me. I wanted to cry but I would not allow myself to do so. If I could just hang on, when the moon rose again I would eat my fill and then head for Mother and home. Even as I reasoned, grave doubts troubled my mind. I seemed to be all alone. I had no idea which way I should go. I could search for many nights and still be no nearer to Mother. I was lost and alone. In spite of my determination, a tear slid from my eye and dripped on my paw. Then a bluejay screamed, scolding someone for some wrong done. It was a welcome sound. Creatures did live in the forest after all. I sniffed back my tears and curled up to sleep.

Chapter Four

I slept soundly throughout that day. I think that I must have tossed and turned in my sleep, for my hard bed looked to have been scuffed and scraped when I awoke. Again I was stiff and sore. I stretched my muscles and tried to flex the pain from them. It didn't work. I knew that I would just have to live with it. Cautiously, I left my den with the foolish hope that my breakfast might be waiting just outside the door. I didn't want to frighten it away before I had the opportunity to enjoy it. There was nothing there.

I did have one pleasant surprise. Two bush rabbits were playing a game of tag not far from my log. I hurried forward eagerly, hoping to make their acquaintance; but at a sharp thump from their mother's hind feet, their heads snapped up and they quickly darted for cover. A sadness filled me. I had so wanted to talk to them. Why had they hurried off? It was almost as though they were purposely avoiding me. Surely not! I had done nothing to offend them. Unless, of course, I had unknowingly slept in their den. Perhaps I should find another log. I didn't want any

misunderstandings with my new neighbors—especially when I needed their help to find my way home. But first, I needed to find something to eat and drink.

I started off, my nose working as I went. I really didn't have very high hopes I'm afraid, but I hadn't gone far when I thought that I smelled water. I kept on going. Yes, very definitely, it was water. I hurried on. I had to shift my direction some as I was headed a little to the north of the water, and might have missed it entirely had I not discovered my error. When I did get my bearings I found a small creek. It was a welcome sight. I busied myself with finding a spot where I could reach the water without taking a bath at the same time. There was a rather well-worn path to the water's edge and I proceeded along it. By stretching, being careful not to lean too far, I was just able to reach my tongue to the freshness of the water. How good it was to find water! And so close to my den, as well. Then I reminded myself that as I would soon be going home again, I wouldn't need this water supply. Well, it's nice to know anyway, I told myself, just in case I don't go for another night.

Because of the clouds in the sky, the moon did not light the path well. I had to travel almost totally by smell and instincts. It was difficult for me, though I felt sure that Mother could have managed it with no problem. I followed the creek and came to a small pond. It was very nice, but I really didn't have time to stand admiring it.

I must find some food, I told myself and began to move away. A big splash sounded almost at my very feet. Another followed a short distance away. I stood stock still, listening. Not a sound reached me through the stillness. I did not so much as quiver. After some minutes, into the silence came a "croak." It was soon joined by another, and another, and another. From all sides of me the chorus seemed to come. Frogs! I remembered my first night out with Mother. That night we had feasted on frogs. They were delicious. Here I had my breakfast as well as my water.

I smiled to myself in the darkness and thought of how good it was going to be to have a full tummy after what seemed like such a long, long time of putting up with an empty one. I moved slightly to better position myself for the feast and heard splashes all around me. The croaking ceased. I waited. The frogs waited. I thought that they would never croak again. At last one did, but I could tell by the sound that he was way across the pond from me. It seemed a long way around to him, but I started out. By the time I had reached the other side of the pond, three or four others had joined him in his night song. I headed for what sounded like the biggest one. Just before I reached him, there was a big splash.

It was me. In my hurry to get to the frog, I had failed to notice the sharp drop of the bank. Following my splash there were many other splashes. I crawled disgustedly from the water, shaking my coat noisily. The frogs remained silent. I was annoyed at myself for getting all wet. I didn't like the feel of the wetness or the extra weight that it gave my fur. Busily I went about trying to shake the water from me.

At the same time I waited for the frogs to begin croaking again. Time went on and they still did not make a sound. I decided to stand very still and listen. It took a few minutes but at last it happened. There was a croak, and another, and another, but now they were coming from the *other* side of the pond.

I heaved a heavy sigh and started back around. I traveled the whole distance, only to be greeted with splashes just before I arrived where the frogs had been singing. Again I was forced to wait, and again when the frogs began their song, they were on the other side of the pond.

Reluctantly I started out again. Only splashes. I waited. More songs, another trip, and more splashes. I was getting very hungry by now. The trips around the pond were not only making me hungry but angry as well. Back and forth I went to be met by splashes and then silence. Not a frog moved or stirred near me. I finally realized that I was losing in this bid for breakfast, and I turned my back upon the whole bunch of them and left the pond. They serenaded me as I marched off, but I was not going to be charmed into going back. I was sure that with each croak they must be laughing.

Since frogs were not to be my breakfast, what would be? I decided to try for something that couldn't swim. It seemed that my best bet would be another berry patch. I sniffed at the air to see if I could detect one. I could smell nothing that seemed worth eating. I trudged on, sticking my nose into places where I thought a part of my meal might be. Generally, I was disappointed, though I did find a few crickets and an occasional grub.

I was about to give up when I stumbled unexpectedly across an exciting discovery—the remains from someone's picnic lunch. There were crusts from sandwiches, two apple cores, a banana peel, some crumbs from a tasty cake, and a whole slice of watermelon. It was like a feast. By the time I was finished, I was quite satisfied. I decided to stop by the pond for another drink and then head for my log. It was much too late now to start for home. Anyway, I still had not found someone to ask for help with directions.

As I neared the pond, the frogs stopped croaking and began to dive into the water with even bigger splashes than before. It didn't bother me one bit. My tummy was full and I was content. They could sit there quietly for as long as they wanted. They weren't bothering me any. Just to be contrary, I waited until there was a deep croak right beside me, followed by another on my other side, and then I reached out and splashed the water hard. Frantic leaps exploded all around me, and the splashes in the pool were like a sudden rainstorm. I grinned in the darkness and trudged on home to my log.

Chapter Five

My bed was no more comfortable on my second night in the log. I twisted and turned in an effort to find a way to rest. It seemed that there was always a knot or a twig poking in my side or jabbing at my back. It occurred to me that if I were to use the log for many nights, I should certainly do something about softening my bed. I would not be here long, however, so I didn't see much point in spending time on it. I curled up and made myself as comfy as possible and closed my eyes, ignoring the sharpness that cut into me. I did eventually get to sleep in spite of it, and the next thing I knew the air was cooling and my stomach was telling me that it was time to stir myself again.

I headed directly for the pond. I knew that it held a good supply of creek-fed water. It also had frogs—but I intended to completely ignore them. I was determined to find my breakfast as quickly as possible. Then I could devote the rest of my time to looking for an animal who would give me directions to help me find Mother and the family.

The water was there for the taking, and I drank my fill and then turned my back on the noisy chorus in the pond. I hadn't forgotten how good a meal of frogs tasted, but neither had I forgotten my humiliation of the night before in trying to catch one. I would content myself with grubs, crickets, and berries.

The hunting did not go well. It took me half of the night to find five grubs and three crickets. My stomach was still complaining when the moon moved far to the west. To make matters worse, the clouds that had been threatening all night long, now began to bathe the world with a steady drizzle of cold rain. I knew that my coat would shed a certain amount of water, but I did not want to return to my bed wet to the skin. I headed back for my log. I was still hungry and I had failed to get close enough to another inhabitant of the forest to ask my way home. I had seen three bush rabbits at a distance. I called to them, but they just looked over their shoulders at me and hurried off. I also saw an owl, but he was much too busy hunting for his meal to pay any heed to me.

I returned to the log shortly before the sun was due to get up, and settled myself. I did so wish that my bed was softer. It would not do now to go looking for materials to help the situation. Everything available would be soaking wet. Again I longed for Mother's warm and comfortable bed and the security of her presence with me. If Mother were with me, I felt quite confident that I would not have been going to bed hungry. I put the thought from my mind and concentrated on sleep.

It was my hunger that awakened me. As I looked out from the shelter of my log, I could see that it was still raining. I hated to start off in the rain but I did need something to eat. I headed again for the pond and a drink of water.

Even before I got to the pond, I became excited.

Hunting in the rain wasn't so bad after all. There seemed to be an abundance of crawly things that made a delightful breakfast. Mind you, it took an awful lot of them to make a mouthful, but they did add up. I didn't dare pass them by as I went for my drink, because I knew full well that they might not be around when I decided to return for them. Therefore I walked slowly, checking carefully about me on the path as I went. It took me a long time to reach the pond. By then I was thoroughly soaked but, though I shivered, I chose to ignore *that* discomfort in my excitement of caring for my *other* discomfort—my gnawing, complaining tummy. I took a quick drink and continued on with my hunting.

I had not gone far when I saw a hedgehog. He too was busy looking for his breakfast. I was so excited to see him that I had to check myself to keep from calling out excitedly. I did hasten my steps, however; and by the time I approached him, I was almost on the run.

He looked up suddenly and his eyes widened. He backed off a few steps and, at the look on his face, I slowed down. Suddenly he wheeled around; and even before I could say a "How-do-you-do" or ask regarding my mother, he was gone. I felt like crying as I watched him go. What was the matter with everyone? Why wouldn't they talk to me? Or was it that there was something the matter with me? I didn't feel like any more breakfast. I wasn't completely full, but I was wet and lonesome and miserable. I decided to head for the log.

As I entered the log and headed for my corner within its depths, a feeling of being "home" came over me. Even though I did not have Mother or the family, or even any friends, the uncomfortable knots and lumps of the log seemed to welcome me. At least here I felt safe and, in a strange way, even at home. I decided that if the rain was over by evening, I would find some suitable material for making myself a warm, cozy bed. Maybe I would need to stay a few more nights in the log after all.

Chapter Six

By night it had stopped raining, but everything was still very wet. I knew that it would be useless to try to fix my bed, so I started out for the pond instead. I was hungry. I had not eaten enough the night before. In fact, there had been only one night since I had left my mother that I had really had enough to eat. I hoped to do better. Surely there must be plenty of food in the forest. Even before I reached the pond, I could hear the frogs croaking; then suddenly there was total silence. Then the song resumed. Then a splash, followed by many other splashes, and again silence. As I stood listening, this was repeated over and over. My curiosity drew me on. I knew that I was too far away to be the reason for the recurrence of silence, then song. I was rushing forward rather clumsily when I burst forth from the undergrowth. There were many splashes.

"Ya dumb kid," said an angry voice. There on a fallen tree by the edge of the pond was a large angry-looking raccoon.

I stopped short.

"Look what you did," he went on. "I almost had the biggest one of the bunch when you came charging out like you had no sense in your head and scared them all out of their wits. They likely won't show their heads again all night now."

He sort of hissed in disgust and leaped away from the tree limb, disappearing in the undergrowth. I never even got a chance to say that I was sorry.

I *was* sorry. I had no idea that my noise could scare away someone's potential breakfast. How was I to know that dumb ol' frogs didn't care for the racket? They wouldn't show again all night, the mad coon had declared. But that was wrong. Why, I had chased back and forth half of one night making lots of noise and scaring them into the water again and again, and they had still kept showing up. Oh, it took them a while, to be sure, but they still appeared. How was I to know that frogs didn't like noise?

Suddenly it hit me. Perhaps that had been my trouble. Maybe when one hunted frogs, one had to be extremely quiet. I decided to try it. Standing motionless and waiting in absolute silence nearly got to me. My legs began to twitch and my whole body asked to be allowed to move, but I made myself stay under control. I didn't like this way of hunting for my breakfast, but if that's what it took I determined to stick it out.

It seemed forever before a frog began to croak, but he was way across the pond from me. I knew from previous experience that it would do no good for me to go running around to try to find him, so I argued with myself to stay put. Soon another frog began to croak, and then another and another, and each one of them seemed to be just a little nearer to where I stood. Finally, only a few feet to my right, another began. I strained my eyes and ears in the darkness. A head appeared. The frog did not even

seem to notice me as he joined heartily in the song. As he croaked he even swam a little, and his swimming was bringing him nearer and nearer to me.

I could hold still no longer. Already I was tasting the delicacy that he would be. I jumped at him, my paws outstretched to scoop him out of the water. I missed! I missed completely and, with a startled croak and a big splash, the frog was gone—and so were all of his brothers and sisters, aunts and cousins. Not a head was seen nor a croak was heard. I left the pond then. The coon could have the whole bunch of them for all that I cared. It didn't work—whether you made a lot of racket or stood as still as a statue. A frog was still a frog!

I did my breakfasting elsewhere that night. The grass was dripping and the path wet with tiny puddles. There were still grubs and other creeping things about. It took a long time to gather enough food to ease my hunger; and then, because the sun was about due to make an appearance, I headed for the log.

I had not gone far when I heard a slight stirring in the bushes ahead of me. I had learned my lesson with Mr. Raccoon, so this time I crept forward very cautiously. Two coyotes were playing in the undergrowth. They were still in the cub stage, and as they romped and tussled I could hardly refrain from joining them. Some friends at last! Eagerly I moved out to make their acquaintance. I had failed to notice their mother lying a few feet from where they were playing, but I saw her quickly enough when I heard her sharp "yip" and saw her spring to her feet. She spoke sharply to her young and they whirled away to follow her. Before I scarce had time to draw a breath, all three of them had disappeared.

I trudged on home. It appeared that I was to have no friends in this new forest. I crawled into my hollow log and attempted to go to sleep. My stomach still rumbled a bit; again I was tired and wet. But the most miserable feeling of all was the feeling of loneliness. If only I had someone to talk to. I curled up in a tight ball and allowed myself to shed some tears. I felt somewhat better after my good cry, and I snuggled down and closed my eyes in sleep.

Chapter Seven

I had resigned myself to being a loner. It was plain to me that no one in the forest wished to make friends with me. Although I couldn't understand it, I guessed that I would need to just accept it and carry on alone.

I arose a bit early the next night because I was determined to make my bed while the materials at hand were nice and dry. I busied myself carrying leaves and moss and tried to arrange it in the fashion that Mother had. I never could get it to go quite right, but at least there was some improvement.

After I was satisfied that I had done what I could, I set out for the pond again. I drank my fill and then was subjected to the splash of frogs as they seemed to tease me from their safe refuge in the pond's watery shallows. I licked my chops thinking of what a delightful meal they would make.

They must have felt that they knew me and knew also that I was really no threat to their safety, for they hardly waited until I finished my drink before they began to croak again. Some of them were very near to me, and I felt an anger rise up within me. Instead of moving on, I stood motionless. As difficult as it was, I waited patiently until a croaking frog swam very near to me. With all of the energy that I could muster, I sprang right at him. There was a big splash as I hit the water. The frog's splash followed it closely, along with many other splashes all around the pond.

I crawled out and shook my wet coat. Then I headed down the path to the old berry patch. Perhaps there would be a few new berries on the bushes.

The berry picking was slim. I only found a few, and what I did find were small and green. They were not very good eating. I did find some crickets and a few other bugs. I was feeling dejected when I remembered the leftovers from the picnic lunch that I had found. I didn't suppose there was a chance that I could be that lucky twice, but it wouldn't hurt to check it out. I headed for the spot.

To my delight I found that there had been another picnic. In fact, maybe several picnics. I also found that there were other animals who had decided to take advantage of the fact. Two coons were scrapping over a large barrel that seemed to be filled with good things. A possum was enjoying himself in a smaller barrel closer to me. I watched them in silence, knowing that they weren't very likely to share. They were still busily engaged when a large bear, followed closely by two young cubs, came around the end of the picnic table. The coons did not even fight for their rights. At one grunt from that big bear, they surrendered the barrel without a fuss. The possum, too, disappeared. It seemed that there would be more food there than the bear and her cubs needed now that the others had all gone. I didn't intend to cut in on her digging and rooting in the large barrel but I didn't think that she would mind if I just checked out the smaller one. I approached very quietly, not wanting to disturb her or her quarreling cubs.

I was almost to the small barrel when her head swung up and her nose began to busily sniff the wind. With one alarmed "woof," she swung away from the barrel and was gone, her two cubs scurring along in an effort to keep up with her. I don't know what it was that made her decide to leave. I guessed that it was just me again. I did hope that I hadn't offended her in any way, and then I decided to forget all about her and just go to work on my meal. In her haste to rush off, she had tipped the big barrel over on its side, which was a big help to me. I could walk right in and thoroughly go over its contents.

My, there were a lot of good things there. I couldn't believe my find. I tasted things that night that I had never tasted before. By the time I decided to head for my log, my tummy was bulging. My feet dragged. My eyes felt heavy. If there is anything that makes one feel sleepy, it's a full tummy. I could hardly wait to reach my bed.

The log looked so inviting when I finally reached it. I pushed my way in. At the narrow door my tummy rubbed against the sides, it was so full. I reached my bed and flopped down. The soft leaves and moss were a real improvement in the comfort of my bed, even if they weren't arranged just right. Eventually I would get them worked around to just where I wanted them.

I tried to curl up, but my full tummy prevented me from becoming much of a ball. Instead I just tucked my feet in a bit and snuggled down with my head lying on a pile of soft leaves. Contentedly I sighed, then grinned in the darkness. How nice to have a full pond and barrels full of picnic leftovers so close at hand. And how nice it was of the big mama bear and her two young cubs to be so willing to share.

Chapter Eight

I slept all day, hardly stirring or shifting position in my sleep. When I awoke, I was surprised to find that I actually felt hungry again. I yawned, stretched, and worked the sleep-kinks from my muscles. My soft bed felt so good that for one moment I was tempted to just turn over and go right back to sleep again. Instead I stirred myself, knowing that if I didn't go out for breakfast I would be feeling starved before another moon rose to cover the earth with its soft light.

When I pushed my nose out of the log entrance, I found a cool and pleasant evening beckoning me. I moved forward cautiously. Mama's training—in fact the very first lesson—had taught us to advance only after having carefully tested to determine that no danger lay in our pathway.

Feeling my confidence grow as I moved down the path, I hurried my footsteps toward the pool. In fact, I even broke into a rather lopsided lope, my tail pluming out behind me.

The pool was a busy place. Across the way I could see a

raccoon washing his breakfast before eating. A fish jumped, sending out ripples that were caught in the light of the moon. The frogs farthest away from the action were giving an occasional croak and a splash here and there. I paused to drink, enjoying the coolness of the water as it trickled down my throat. I liked the pool, and yet I was quite willing to share it with the other creatures of the forest.

I was turning to head for the picnic area when I noticed a pair of eyes studying me. They belonged to a huge bullfrog. Another frog nearby croaked out a warning, and I caught the conversation between them.

"Don't you think that you should take cover?" asked the smaller frog, to which the big one replied, "Naw—it's just that dumb skunk again. He'll starve to death before he'll make a hunter. All we need to do is sit tight for a moment and he'll get tired and leave."

I turned my back on them but it did bother me some. Well, let them croak on; I didn't care. I could get a good breakfast from the picnic barrels.

I was leaving in a bit of a huff when I noticed that the coon had moved around to my side of the pond. Remembering how angry he had become with me when I had frightened away his breakfast before, I stopped right where I was, making not a breath of sound nor a shiver of movement. I watched him. He, too, was motionless—and silent. He stood poised, until I thought that surely he must have frozen to the spot. The frogs soon resumed their song, seeming to pick up the tune right where they had left off. There was an occasional splashing or diving as frogs visited or lunched or just exercised a bit.

Suddenly the coon moved, one silent quick movement; and when his paw came up out of the water, it held a frog for his breakfast. Even the frogs nearby scarcely saw the movement or heard the sound. Only a few even stopped singing and those who did didn't even bother to splash back into the depths of the pond. So that was how it was done! I filed the information in the back of my mind just in case I should ever need it. For the time, I would still enjoy the tasty treats of the barrels and I headed in that direction. I don't believe that the coon had even spotted me. At least I did not hear him snarl angrily in my direction. I decided to practice moving very quietly through the woods.

I must have practiced well, for I was almost on the very tails of two bush bunnies before they noticed me. I was all set to stop for a visit but they darted off into the underbrush. A big sigh escaped me. Would I ever be able to make friends in this new neighborhood?

The barrels were already occupied. Two possums were arguing over the contents of one of them. I couldn't understand for the life of me why they should be fighting. There was plenty for everyone. I moved over to the second barrel to ask an overweight raccoon if he'd mind sharing it with me. He left me the whole thing and went off into the woods muttering to himself.

I had decided not to let it bother me and went right to work on the first course. The food was plentiful and tasty, and I soon had filled my little tummy again.

It was early, and I didn't feel like going back to my log. I still wasn't sleepy. I decided to go for a walk instead.

I headed off in a direction that I had never taken before. The path was well-worn, so I felt sure that a number of the woodland residents must live over that way. Sure enough, I had not gone far when I met some bush rabbits. They did not stay to talk or play, so I continued down the path. I saw a mother coon who was busy scolding her offspring. One of the bold little fellows answered her back and got a sharp slap for his brashness. I thought that it wasn't very likely that either of them would be in the mood for a neighborly chat, so I detoured around them and hurried on down the path.

After going some distance, I came upon a meadow. It was lovely by moonlight. The slight breeze stirred the fragrant flowers, making them wave and dance in unison. Here and there crickets chirped, and small night creatures stirred the grasses underfoot. A large owl swooped through the neighboring branches and then rested on a limb, filling the night with his strange cry. Another owl answered him from somewhere in the distance. I couldn't help but wish that my log were here in this meadow. It was alive with woodland folk.

Very near to me there was a stirring, and I turned my head. There, only a few feet away, stood a fawn, daintily nibbling on some delicate grasses. I held my breath, watching her. She was quite the most graceful creature that I had ever seen. I stood quietly. I did not want her to run away. Suddenly she lifted her head and looked right at me. I did not speak or move, though I wanted to with all of my heart. Then the most amazing thing happened. She smiled.

"Hello," she said shyly.

"Hello," I echoed, hardly above a whisper.

"Are you new here?"

I nodded my head in assent.

"Do you live in the meadow?"

I found my tongue then. "No, I live that way—in my log house."

I was just going to ask her where she lived, when her mother moved into view. She stopped short and looked at me, then at her baby, and then back to me. She was slim and graceful as she stood statue-like in the moonlight, but the look on her face was one of concern, not pleasure.

"Come, dear," she said rather sharply. Though I wanted to protest, the young fawn did not for a moment question her mother, and the two of them quickly left me and I

could hear them leaving the meadow, also.

I decided to leave then, too. All of the joy had gone out of my venture. I took my full tummy and headed for my log. It was some distance back, and I knew that by the time I reached it I would be sleepy and ready for bed.

Even as I trudged along I had visions of the lithe, young fawn. It would be so nice to have her for a friend. Maybe if I visited the meadow, I would see her again. I decided to get the business of eating over as quickly as possible the next night so that I would have plenty of time to spend in the meadow.

Chapter Nine

I did not see the fawn in the meadow the next night, nor the next, nor the next. I had almost given up, but I still turned my feet back toward the meadow the next night also. The meadow was such a pleasant place to be that I enjoyed my time there, even if it did mean that I spent it all alone.

The night was a beautiful one. I couldn't remember seeing such a multitude of stars, nor seeing them as bright and seemingly close at hand. There was not even the slightest breeze. The calls and cries, chirps and croaks of the night people were all around me. Instead of making me feel a part of my beautiful world, somehow the awareness that there were so many fellow creatures so nearby made me feel a deep-stirring loneliness. I tried to push it away from me and enjoy the scents and the sounds, but it was not to be dealt with so easily.

Suddenly, the tranquility of the night was shattered. It was not a sound as much as it was a feeling. Without knowing why, I knew that something was wrong—terribly wrong. Then I heard a rushing, as frantic feet raced toward me. I ran—as quickly as I could run—down the path to where there was a sharp rise so that I might get a better look as to what the commotion was about.

When I saw what was happening, it took a minute for me to understand. There was my new fawn friend and she was running wildly, as though absolutely terrified and there, fast on her flying heels, was a full grown coyote. When it finally got through to me that the coyote was after his breakfast, my heart began to pound within my chest. The coyote was gaining. Even I could see that. Then he reached for her and just as I was sure that my eyes were to behold a scene of horror, the fawn veered sharply and the coyote missed. On they went, and again I watched the same thing happen. Again and again. But the fawn was tiring. It was easy to see that she wouldn't be able to keep up her evasive maneuvers much longer.

There was another sound and I whirled around to see the fawn's mother running forward. Her eyes looked terror-filled and a slight sound escaped from her throat. I was so relieved to see her that I could have cried. There wasn't much time, I knew, and it appeared to me that the mother must move quickly to save her young. She didn't move forward to attack the coyote as I had expected her to. Instead, with fear making her whole body tremble, she moved out into the open and began to run and stumble right before the eyes of the coyote. I realized that she was hoping to divert him from her young and get him to chase her instead. It didn't work. The coyote stayed with his original quarry. He, too, must have realized full well that the fawn was too tired to continue running much longer. Then a strange thing happened. The fawn stopped her weaving and darting and ran directly down the path. Terror must have made her forsake the only defense that she had.

They were coming directly toward me. I knew that the

coyote could almost taste his breakfast. Oh, how I ached to help—to do something to deliver my new little friend from the jaws so close behind her. But what could such an animal as I do that a large animal like her mother couldn't—and against a fierce animal like a coyote?

A strange feeling passed through my body. Maybe there was a way—a way that I had not even been aware of, for some inner instinct was trying to tell me something.

I let the fawn pass by and then whirled sharply, stamped my feet, and threw up my tail. My aim was good. A sharp cry arose from the coyote. He stopped his running and turned back down the path. As he left the meadow he was still yipping and crying, and occasionally he would stop his running to rub at his eyes with his paws and even roll his head in the grass.

I stood motionless, amazed at what had just happened. When I could finally stir, I looked about me. The coyote had completely disappeared but I could still hear his distant yipping. The fawn had collapsed in the tall meadow grasses and her mother had moved over quickly to comfort her with her warm tongue. The air was filled with a pungent, rather objectionable odor. I wrinkled up my nose and moved.

Without thinking, I moved toward the mother and the fawn. When I got within a few feet of them I suddenly realized what I was doing. I stopped. Should I leave? I would so much like to tell them how glad I was that the coyote had left and the baby was safe. But perhaps they did not wish to speak to me—and the baby was far too tired for the mother to say, "Come dear," as she had said before when the fawn had spoken to me. I dared not approach them. Besides, there was a horrid and potent smell hanging heavily in the night air. I sniffed at it, not liking it one bit.

Suddenly, I was aware that the awful smell must have

come from me. My face flushed with shame. What must they think of me? I dared not move lest they would become conscious of the fact that I was still there. Why, I could have asphyxiated the whole lot of us! The dreadfulness of it all filled me with embarrassment. If only I could sneak quietly off before I was noticed. I began to back away, hoping to disappear. The mother lifted her head and saw me. I held my breath, but instead of nuzzling her fawn to her feet so that they could hastily leave, she approached me and there were tears in her eyes.

"How can I ever thank you?" she said in a soft voice. "Oh, if it hadn't been for you, my baby . . ." She couldn't go on. Even the very thought of what would have surely happened made her shiver.

"Thank you," she said again. "Thank you so much. If ever . . . if ever there is anything . . . anything that we can do . . ."

I couldn't believe that she was even willing to speak with me—I mean with the nasty smell and all—and here she was wanting to do something for me in return. I was so desperate that I decided to swallow my pride and plead if need be. I was surprised at my boldness.

"Well—there is one thing," I stammered. The enormity of the thing that I was about to ask frightened me and made me check my tongue. Surely the mother deer hadn't intended to go *that* far.

"Yes?" she prompted me.

I couldn't go on.

"Yes?" she asked again. "Please . . . please continue. I know that there isn't much that I can do, but I promise you that if it's at all in my power . . ."

I gulped and gathered my courage.

"If . . . if it isn't too presumptious . . . I mean . . . if you don't mind too much . . . could . . . could . . .?" I swallowed hard and then blurted it out. "Could we be friends?''

After I had said it, I wished that I hadn't been so bold. What if she turned angrily away—or laughed at my boldness?

But she didn't. Her eyes opened wide in astonishment and then a tender look filled them, and she said with deep meaning, ''Oh, yes . . . yes. For always. Yes. Indeed you are our friend—our most *special* friend.''

Slowly I took in her words; then a grin spread over my face.

''Jiminy Whiz!'' I said excitedly.

I felt like laughing, like shouting, like wagging my tail—but skunks don't do that. I did wave my plume ever so slightly and then, remembering suddenly wherein lay my secret power, I quickly held it still. The air was quite full enough with the dreadful smell.

The mother deer moved back to her fawn.

''Cassandra,'' she said softly, ''We have a new friend. This is . . . I'm sorry, I don't know your name.''

Cassandra raised her head. I noticed that her sides were not heaving as much now. She even managed a slight smile. I smiled back and then I remembered that her mother was still waiting for my name.

''Fuzzle,'' I said.

''This is Fuzzle,'' the mother deer continued, and the way that she spoke my name made it sound pretty.

Cassandra struggled to her feet. I wanted to tell her to stay where she was but even I knew that it would not be wise. There were other dangers in the woods. One must always be on the alert and ready to run if necessary. She still looked shaky but she was brave. Again she smiled.

''Hi, Fuzzle,'' she said, and then she added quietly, ''thank you.''

''Oh, it was nothing,'' I stammered, embarrassed by the whole thing. ''I was so afraid . . .''

"So was I," she said, and she began to tremble again. Her mother wisely changed the topic of conversation.

"Where do you live, Fuzzle?"

"I live in a hollow log down by the creek-bed. Just a little ways down the trail from the pond. The creek is almost dry now over near my log."

"It dries up in the summer heat, but if we get a good rain it will fill again," said Mrs. Deer. "We are very fortunate here in Wonder Meadow that we always have the pond for our water supply."

"Wonder Meadow?" I said. "Is that the name for this beautiful place?"

The deer looked around her with pride in her eyes.

"Yes, this is Wonder Meadow; and it is beautiful, isn't it?"

"I love it," I said frankly. "I wish that my log was over here."

"I don't suppose it could be moved."

"I don't think so. It's pretty big."

"Maybe you could find another log—over here."

"But I've got that one all padded and lined. It's nice. I like it."

"I see," the mother deer said, and I could tell by her eyes that she understood how it was to love one's home.

Cassandra began to move around. She flexed her leg muscles as though testing to see if they would still work. I wondered if she would be stiff and sore after her hard run, but she looked as graceful as ever.

"Are you feeling better?" I asked.

"Oh, much better, thank you, Fuzzle. Why I believe that I could even jump that fallen log over there."

I was afraid that she might try it, and I believe her mother was, too.

"Not for awhile, my dear," she said firmly.

I realized suddenly that the deer might not have

gathered their evening meal as yet.

"I must let you go," I said to them. "I'm sure that you have things to do before the sun comes up."

"Well, I do believe that if Cassandra feels quite ready for it, we should continue our feeding on the meadow grass. We still must make our way to the pond as well before we retire."

"Will I see you again?" I asked quickly, not wanting them to go away.

"Oh, yes. We will watch for you. We feed here in the meadow almost every night." Then with big smiles and calls to one another of "Be seeing you," we parted our ways.

I headed back to my log home, almost silly with happiness. I had a friend—my first real friend. I was no longer all alone. I had a friend. No, that was not right. I had *two* friends.

Chapter Ten

When I awakened the next night, I was so excited that I didn't know what I should do first. It had been my practice to go first to the pond and then to the picnic area. But that was before I had friends. Now it was hard to know what was the most important thing for me to do—care for my hungry tummy or go to see my friends. I finally got myself under control and decided to take care of my breakfast as usual. I headed first for the pond.

Two raccoons were hunting. One was the big fellow that I had seen there many times before. I was careful to walk quietly so that he wouldn't be annoyed and snarl at me. I was surprised when he looked my way and gave a definite nod of greeting. In fact, I was so surprised that I almost fell right into the water from which I was drinking.

I finished my drink and was moving off when the other coon noticed me.

"Hi, Fuzzle," he called and frogs all around him splashed into the water. I held my breath, expecting the big raccoon to really give the young fellow a piece of his mind, but he said nothing. I called, "Hi," rather weakly in return, hoping that I wouldn't scare any more frogs and hurried off down the trail.

The farther I traveled, the more perplexed I became. The raccoon had called to me and he had actually sounded friendly, and even the big, grouchy raccoon had not scolded or complained. It was a puzzle—a real puzzle.

When I reached the picnic area, heads lifted at my approach. A bear and her cubs eyed me, then moved a little further away; but they didn't make a run for it. The possum was openly friendly.

"Hi, Fuzzle," he called, "there's lots of good stuff in this barrel. Want to join me?"

I was too shocked to even reply, but I moved over to join him at his barrel. He was right. There was a lot of good stuff there.

After eating my fill, I thanked him and turned to the path leading to Wonder Meadow. I was so anxious to see Cassandra and her mother that I could hardly wait.

As I hurried along, two bush rabbits crossed the path. They were still shy but they did greet me with a subdued "Hi." I answered their greeting, trying not to sound as surprised as I felt.

When I reached the meadow the moon was casting long shadows across the gently waving meadow growth. The flowers danced and the crickets serenaded. It was beautiful in the meadow.

I immediately looked around for Cassandra. There was no evidence of any animals anywhere. For a moment I thought that I was to spend the entire evening alone again, when suddenly the whole meadow came alive.

"Surprise . . . surprise!" rang out all around me, and from behind every bush and out of every hole came woodland people. "Surprise . . . surprise, Fuzzle!" they called laughingly.

I stood dumb-struck.

Cassandra came up to me with a twinkle in her eye. "Do you like it? Your friends are giving you a party."

"A party?"

"Yes. A welcoming party. We want to welcome you to Wonder Meadow and to Looking-glass Pond and to Pleasant Woods. We want you to know that we are glad that you have come to be our new neighbor."

I couldn't believe my ears nor the words of the folks who crowded about me wanting to make sure that I knew that I was welcome in their midst. I felt intense embarrassment. It was apparent that my new neighbors had heard the report of my rescue of Cassandra, but had they heard *how* I had chased off the coyote? Would they really want me for a friend if they knew? I decided to say nothing about it and to make sure that I didn't embarrass myself —or them—with my secret weapon again.

We spent the entire remainder of the evening playing games and chatting, and then, just before the sun was about to waken the morning world, we had lunch together. The small coon, named Ringo, produced a *whole* apple that he had found in the barrel—just for me. I ate until my sides bulged. The sun was climbing over the eastern horizon when we finally pulled ourselves away. Amid shouts and cries to one another we headed for our beds, leaving by various trails that headed into the forest.

I could still hardly believe that it had actually happened! Cassandra and her mother had spread the word quickly about the events of the night before and encouraged all of the woodland people to make me feel welcome in their neighborhood. Well, they had certainly made me feel welcome all right. In fact, I felt that I was even *special*— a feeling that was very new to me. The deer family must have guarded my awful secret well.

A squirrel met me on the trail. Squirrels, being day creatures, and I seldom meet. I wasn't sure what this fellow would do now. He didn't go out of his way to pat me on the back or anything, but he did give me a curt nod; and when I smiled in return, he actually stopped and said that it had all the makings of a fine day. I agreed heartily and stumbled on toward my bed. I was sleepy from the night of merrymaking, and my tummy was still full with the meal of the night—plus the special dessert of the apple.

I pushed my way into my log. My sides bumped against the sides of the entrance, and I knew that if I put on much more weight it would be quite a squeeze. I reached my bed and sniffed around it to make sure that everything was just as I had left it. It was. I sighed contentedly and then flopped down on the softness of the leaves and moss. Oh, how good it felt. And how good I felt. I had Looking-glass Pond to be a constant water supply, Pleasant Woods Camp Ground for all of my shopping needs, and Wonder Meadow to meet with all of my friends. I, Fuzzle, had friends—not just one friend or two friends, but many, many friends. Why, there were so many that I hadn't even bothered to count! I closed my eyes, smiled to myself, and prepared for the best dream that I had ever enjoyed in my life.

Chapter Eleven

I couldn't wait to get with my new friends again. When I awoke the next night, I hardly waited for my eyes to open before I left the log. I started for the pond in a lopsided lope. The night air smelled cool and the clouds completely covered the moon. A strong wind was blowing, bringing with it the scent of a coming storm. Ordinarily I would have been cautious as I ventured forth, but tonight I was in far too much of a hurry. I rushed around a bend in the path and nearly ran headlong into a woodland creature coming my way. I did not know this animal and as I braked to a stop and prepared to greet him, a funny thing happened right before my eyes. Suddenly his fur stuck straight up, with long spindles pointing toward the sky. He looked like a round ball completely covered with long white pine needles. I skidded to a quick halt.

We stood and looked at one another for a moment. Neither of us moved.

"Hi," I finally ventured. "I don't believe that I know you. I'm Fuzzle."

As I spoke, the long sharp spines began to lower slightly

and a small face appeared.

"Hi," answered a squeaky voice.

"I've never seen you before," I continued.

"I don't come over this way often."

"What did you say your name was?"

The needles were completely down now, blending in once again with his fur.

He giggled and the giggle too was squeaky.

"I didn't say, but my name is Cuddles."

"Cuddles?"

"That's right. I live over on the other side of the meadow in the grove of tall trees."

"How'd you do that?" I asked suddenly, too awed by what had happened to give much consideration to politeness.

"What?"

"That. Make your fur all full of those pine needles."

"Those aren't pine needles."

"They're not?"

"No, those are *my* needles."

"Your needles?"

"Right." He giggled again.

"Where'd you get 'em?" I asked, still mystified.

"Where'd I get 'em?"

"Yeah. They're neat. I'd kinda like to get me a bunch, too."

"You don't have any, huh?"

"Me?" I indicated my black and white coat. "No, I don't have anything like that. Where'd you get yours?"

"The Maker gave them to me."

"The Maker?" This was all very new and strange to me. "What Maker?"

"Why the Creator of all things—birds and flowers, sky and pond, animals and—well, everything."

"You, too?"

"Sure," Cuddles squeaked, "and you, too."

I had never heard of the Maker before. I was still puzzling over it when Cuddles spoke again.

"What did He give you?"

"What do you mean?" I asked him, perplexed.

"Well, what did He give you? He gave all of His creatures some special means of protection. What did He give you?"

"I don't know," I said honestly. I had never thought of it before. "Maybe . . . maybe . . . do you think that He forgot? I mean, I don't have anything like that at all."

"No," said Cuddles quite confidently, "He didn't forget. He gave you something special—for sure."

I just shrugged my shoulders.

"Well, let's see," went on Cuddles. "Do you have strong legs for running fast?"

I thought of my rather ungainly trot and shook my head.

"Nope," I answered, sure that that wasn't my specialty.

"Well, can you change color to fit in with the changing seasons?"

Again I looked at myself.

"I've never seen me any way else but black and white," I answered.

"Let me see," said Cuddles. "Do you have strong front feet and teeth for digging quickly?"

I had never dug anything more than the soft dirt around an ant hill, or under a log or stone.

"Nope," I said again.

"Well, do you have special claws for climbing trees?"

I laughed. Though I had never tried it, I was quite sure that it wouldn't work if I did.

"No," I said, "I can't do that."

"Well, you're not very big," said Cuddles, "so size can't be your protection." Cuddles shrugged, "Well, it beats me,'' he said, ''but just the same I'm sure that He didn't forget you. Someday—someday when you need it—you'll discover something.''

''Hey,'' I cried, excitement filling me through and through. ''I know! Just the other night my friend Cassandra was in real trouble and I . . . I . . .'' I hardly knew how to say it. It seemed like rather a delicate subject, but Cuddles was waiting. ''Well,'' I went on rather lamely, ''all of a sudden I realized that . . . that . . . I sprayed,'' I blurted out. ''Right in the face of the coyote, I sprayed.''

''Did it work?'' asked Cuddles and he sounded as excited as I had.

''Boy, did it work!'' I exclaimed. ''He ran off shrieking and clawing and rubbing his face in the dirt. I think that the spray must have stung his eyes. We never did see him again.''

''You see,'' said Cuddles triumphantly, ''the Maker did give you something special!''

It was a sobering thought and a rather exciting one as well. To think that this special something that I had, had come directly from the Maker, for *me*.

''You think so? I mean do you really think that He . . .?''

''Of course. Of course,'' squeaked Cuddles.

''But why? I mean why did He . . .? Why did He make me *special*?''

''Because He cares about you!''

''Me?'' it was hard to believe that the Maker of the stars, the moon, the wind, the animals, everything, would care about me.

''Of course He does. He loves all of His creatures. Every one of us. That's why He was careful to give each one of us some means of protecting ourselves.''

I thought of my friends. Cassandra had been swift and evasive when the coyote had been chasing her. If it had not been for her strong legs and her agility, she surely would have been caught. The bears had size as their protection; and, I was told by the oppossum, they also had very keen noses. The squirrels could climb quickly and be out of reach in the whisk of a tail. The rabbits had swiftness of feet as well as coats that changed colors. Benjy had been boasting to me about the sparkling white that her fur became in the winter. Now it was a gray-brown. You could hardly spot her or her brothers and sisters unless you knew where they were hiding, and hide-and-seek was a favorite game of theirs. I thought of each one of my friends. And, yes, it was true. All of them had been given a means of defense.

"Wow," was all that I was able to say. I decided right then and there that if the Maker had given me the special strong scent that had chased off the coyote, and had made me with this special defensive ability, then I would no longer feel shame and embarrassment concerning it. After all, it had been used to save the life of my friend Cassandra. I didn't even waste time wishing that I had been given swift feet, or the ability to climb trees, or a coat that would allow me to hide. I didn't even wish that I had been given the long needles like Cuddles, for I knew that none of those things would have assisted me at the time that I had needed help so desperately—in driving off the coyote. No sirree. My special defense had been the very one that had been effective at the time that help was needed. I felt a great deal of gratitude to the Maker for His choice. I even felt just a small amount of self-pride. I had used my defense—and used it well.

My thoughts returned to Cuddles. "Would you do it again?" I asked him.

He looked puzzled.

"Do what?"

"Make your pine needles stand up straight."

"They're not pine needles," he giggled. "They're *my*

needles.''

''Right,'' I corrected myself. ''Make 'em stand up—please?''

Cuddles did. There in a flash was the needle-covered ball where Cuddles had just been.

I moved forward eagerly, intending to check them out.

''Careful,'' he cried, stepping back a pace. I stopped in my tracks.

''I wasn't going to hurt you,'' I assured him. ''I just wanted to—''

''Well, I might have hurt *you,*'' he cut in.

I just looked at him.

''They're very sharp,'' he explained, ''and a touch of a nose or paw and they can prick you.''

''Really?'' It sounded unreal. ''Jiminy Whiz!''

''Really. In fact one curious bear cub went away with several of my needles stuck in his paw. His mother had to extract them with her teeth. Still he whimpered for hours. I felt sorry for him, but I had tried to warn him; he just wouldn't listen. Next time he meets one of my kind, I'm sure he will be far more careful.''

Cuddles allowed his needles to settle into a less threatening position.

''What *is* your kind?'' I asked him.

''I'm a porcupine,'' he answered with a bit of pride.

''Well, I'm mighty glad that I met you tonight. I'm glad too that you explained to me about our special defenses—and about the Maker.''

''You know,'' squeaked Cuddles, ''I think that you and I have two of the most powerful defenses of any of the woodland creatures.''

I smiled.

''You know, I think you're right,'' I agreed.

''Tell you what,'' went on Cuddles. ''I won't use my defense on you if you don't use your defense on me.''

"It's a deal," I said, laughingly. "Unless of course I see you chasing my friend, Cassandra—"

"Oh, no. Not me. I'm a bark eater. And besides I could never chase anyone. I move too slowly for that."

We moved off together down the trail, visiting as we went. I was pleased to have a friend like Cuddles.

Chapter Twelve

Before I had finished my breakfast, it started to rain. I was going to stay and eat until I was full, but the wetter my coat became the more miserable I was. I finally decided that I had eaten enough and hurried off for home. Before I got halfway, the rain increased and I felt that I would surely wash away if I didn't take cover. I found a fallen log that had formed a shelter of sorts and was well covered with bushes and three growth, and I hurried in. It was dark—and cold—even though it was protected from the heavy rain. I tried to shake some of the rain off my coat but I was soaked too thoroughly to really accomplish much. I pressed toward the back of the shelter in the hopes of finding some warmth, but there was only a hard rock surface and some very cold tree roots.

Oh, how I longed for my own warm bed. I could almost feel the softness and warmth of my leaves and moss in my longing for them. But wishing did not help me. I sat and shivered and tried to keep my teeth from rattling.

I listened carefully for a break in the storm so that I might make a dash for home. The night passed by slowly, chilling minute by chilling minute. I began to wonder if I would ever be warm again.

After some time of shaking and straining to hear the welcome hush of the storm subsiding, I at last decided that there did seem to be a slackening in the rain. I pushed myself forward and stuck my nose out from the shelter. It was still raining but not as heavily as it had been. I decided to run for home as quickly as I could run.

By the time I reached my log, I was again dripping water and chilled clear through. I hurried in and stopped just within my door to get as much of the water from my coat as I could so that I wouldn't soak my bed. I stood dripping and shaking and stroking the water from my fur. It seemed a long time before I was satisfied that I could move forward into my bed. I was still cold. I burrowed down into the leaves and moss and pushed some of the bedding material tightly against my body and tried to quit shaking. It was much later that I realized that I actually was no longer shivering. I still didn't feel warm, but at least I was comfortable enough that I felt like I might be able to go to sleep at last. I curled up even more tightly, snuggled down deeper into the now-warming bed, and closed my eyes.

I felt that I hadn't been asleep for long when I was awakened. At first I couldn't understand why I had roused from my sleep when it was far from time for me to get up. Then I realized that it was noise that had awakened me. That was strange. I was used to noise. The day-creatures were often very noisy, and normally I would sleep right through their commotion. I shook my head at their disturbance. Didn't they realize that there were those who needed sleep?

The noise grew louder and more excited. It was the squirrels. They often fought and chattered and carried on. I couldn't imagine what had them so worked up. I

shifted my position and tried to get back to sleep, but I had barely shut my eyes when I realized that the persistent chattering was now right at my door. I stirred.

"Fuzzle! Fuzzle!" an excited voice cried.

I knew then that it must be more than a neighborhood tiff. I crawled from my warm bed.

"Fuzzle! Fuzzle!" the voice cried again, and this time there was fear as well as excitement in the cry.

"I'm coming. I'm coming," I called as I hurried forward, wondering what in the world could be the matter with them.

Skidder, the big gray squirrel, was already at my door, blocking my view of the outside.

"The rain!" he screamed. "The rain!"

"Is it *still* raining?" I said in exasperation, dreading the thought of hunting for my breakfast in another cold downpour.

"Yes! Yes," he cried, and the creek is flooding!"

"The creek is flooding?" I wondered, as I asked, why this news was of such tremendous import that he should get me out of a sound sleep to inform me.

"Yes. Hurry, hurry!"

All of the squirrels that had gathered around my door began to chatter and call and scold and exclaim at one and the same time. It was a horrible racket.

Skidder hushed them with an angry wave of his tail. "Get back to your homes, all of you," he demanded. "There isn't much time."

I was still bewildered. "Much time for what?"

"To leave. To run. To get to high ground," he babbled.

"Leave? But it's not even evening yet. I don't hunt until—"

He didn't even let me finish. "Not to hunt. To save yourself! And you must hurry. There isn't time to talk."

"What are you talking about?" He backed out of my

doorway, and I moved forward.

"Look!" he cried.

I looked—and there, a few feet from the door of my home, was a rushing angry-looking stream where none had been the day before.

"What . . . what . . .?" I stammered.

"The creek . . . it's flooding!"

"The creek?"

"You must hurry. The water is coming nearer all the time."

He was right. Even in the few minutes that we stood and looked in amazement at the new creek, it appeared that the water was coming closer and closer.

"But what happened?" I persisted.

"I'll explain it later. Now hurry!" He sounded impatient.

I turned for just a moment and looked back at my snug little bed. How I hated to leave it. If the water should continue to climb toward my log, even my warm bed might get soaked. How would I ever get it dry and soft and warm again?

Skidder gave me a nudge and I turned back to him and shook my head in agreement. I was ready to follow where he led. We fled away from the swollen creek and farther up the gradually sloping hill.

Skidder was much faster than I, and my short legs were tired long before he decided that it was safe to quit running.

I was panting and puffing as I was finally allowed to stop to catch my breath. The run hadn't seemed to bother Skidder at all.

"How much farther?" I asked between gasps for air.

"I think you're safe now," he answered. "The water has never reached here."

It was still raining, so one could not see well through the forest. Nor could one hear as well as usual. There was only the drip and splash of countless numbers of raindrops.

''Where are we?'' I panted.

''Up on the side hill. You'll recognize the spot when the sun comes out again.''

''You mean when the sun goes down,'' I smiled. ''I work much better at night time.''

''Excuse me,'' said Skidder, and then laughed. ''That's right,'' he went on, ''I guess we did rather interrupt you at a bad time.''

''It looks like it's a very good thing that you did. I might have been a bit wet before the day was over. Thank you, Skidder.''

Skidder hung his head in embarrassment.

''Aw—that's okay. You saved Cassandra. None of us will ever forget that.''

I realized that Cassandra was very special to the forest people.

''I was glad that I could save Cassandra, even if—even if . . .'' I couldn't finish. For a moment I was silent and then I thought of my talk with Cuddles. ''Well,'' I went on boldly, ''I was mighty glad to discover that the Maker had given me the very defense that would work against the coyote. I guess that I'm one of the few creatures whose defense works for more than just myself, huh?''

''I guess you are,'' said Skidder and he really seemed quite impressed.

''Well, I still want to thank you,'' I said again. I didn't want Skidder to think that I was getting a swelled head about my defense and all. ''If you hadn't come along and warned me, I might have slept until it was too late.''

''What will you do now?'' Skidder asked.

''Well, I do need some more sleep,'' I said. ''So I guess that I will find a spot to curl up in until it is time to properly get up.''

''You can share my nest,'' the neighborly Skidder said.

Before I could even thank him, Skidder's face began to turn red. "On the other hand," he said, "I guess you can't. It's about ten or fifteen feet off the ground."

I laughed, and Skidder lost his embarrassment and joined me. The steadily falling rain began to bother my coat again.

"We've got to get in out of this," I said to Skidder, looking up at the drizzling sky. It didn't look like it ever intended to stop. "I'll find some place. It doesn't really matter too much where. I'll just crawl in someplace where it is dry until it decides to stop raining and I can go home again. You'd better get back inside too, or you're going to be soaked to the skin."

Skidder nodded and we said goodby and he scurried off. Before I turned to look for the dry "somewhere" to spend the rest of the day, I called after Skidder, "And thanks again for the warning, neighbor." Skidder turned, flicked his tail in reply, and was gone.

Chapter Thirteen

I slept through the rest of that day. When I awoke the rain had stopped. I could hardly wait to find out how my log home had fared. As fast as I was able, I hurried toward it. Now that the sun was down and the moon peeked occasionally through the scattered clouds, it was easy for me to get my bearings.

The squirrels had all gone to bed so I wasn't able to find out any other news of the woods from them. I was sure that the heavy rain and flooding creek had caused no harm to their homes, them being so high up in the trees. I did wonder about some of my other friends, but I could think of none of them that lived by the old creekbed near me.

When I reached my part of the woods I could scarcely believe my eyes. The area where my log home was located was completely under water. It certainly was a good thing that Skidder and his friends had called me from my sleep, or I might have been under water, too.

I felt a little sick inside about my home. How long would it be until the creek receded again and I was able to go back to my log? I knew that I would need to take out all of my bedding and put in new dry leaves and moss. Everything in the log would be soaked. I hoped that it would not take too long to dry out. I missed my home. With a deep sigh, I turned from the scene before me and headed for the pond. On the way I met two bush rabbits. Mindy and Mandy were twin daughters of Mrs. R. Rabbit. There were so many rabbits in our woods that they went alphabetically. Mindy called out when she saw me, "Fuzzle. We were worried about you when we heard that the creek had flooded again."

"I'm fine," I hastened to assure her. "Skidder and his family and friends came and woke me."

"And how is your home?"

"It's still under water," I said dejectedly. "I just came from looking at it. It may be a number of days until it is dry enough for me to move back in."

The twin rabbits looked at one another but said nothing.

"Did anyone else have any trouble?" I asked.

"We haven't seen many people yet. We just got up. We were on our way to the pond now."

We walked to the pond together. The path was still wet, and the trees and grasses were dripping. I wondered as I trudged along if our woods would ever be dry again.

When we arrived at the pond, things were in a real commotion. We could hear the uproar before we could see what it was all about. When we did round the bend in the path and beheld the scene before us, we all gasped. Never had we seen the pond as it was at the present. It was twice as big as normal. Water seemed to be everywhere. There was a great deal of hurrying and scurrying, and at first I could not understand what it was all about. Then I realized that it was the beavers who were in such a panic.

"What happened?" I asked a nearby coon who seemed

to be entranced by what was going on.

"The flooding washed away a part of the beaver dam. They are hurrying to repair it before more damage is done."

I could see the problem, once he had pointed it out. Five beavers seemed to be everywhere. Two were carrying large limbs of trees in their mouths and steering them through the water to the rift in the dam. The other three were busy up on the dam, pushing and patting logs, limbs, and mud into place. It looked like a big job to me, and I knew that I wouldn't have even known where or how to start.

"Can they do it?" I asked the coon.

"You better hope that they can," he replied. "Every animal in the forest counts on the pond in one way or another. If we lose it, we are all in trouble."

"You mean we could lose the pond if the beavers don't get the dam fixed?"

"The pond is here *because* of the beaver dam. The water comes from two sources . . . that nearly dry creek there when it rains hard enough and a small creek that feeds in from the other side. The creek only flows heavily when we get hard rains and the water drains in from the nearby hills. The other creek has been dangerously near being dry many times, too. If the beavers hadn't built the dam and filled up the pond at times when there was good rainfall, there would be no water for any of us in the dry seasons. We *all* need that dam—and we need it badly."

"Well," I said, wondering how all of the forest creatures could just stand back and watch the beavers work if the dam was needed by all, "why don't we give them a hand then?"

"Us? Nothing we could do. None of us knows how to build a dam."

"They could show us."

"They're too busy with building to be working with us. We'd just get in their way."

It seemed a shame to me to leave all of the hard work to the poor beavers. I did wish that there was some way to help them out.

As the night went on, more and more creatures gathered on the banks of the pond. There was very little talking for we feared that even our muted conversation might in some way hamper the beavers in their work. Besides, I think that there were those in our number who were afraid of the consequences if the beavers weren't able to stop the flow.

It was near morning before a shout went up from the waiting crowd. I think that the first victory call came from a beaver, in the form of a sharp slap of his tail on the water. Another beaver echoed the splash and then another. At first I thought that something was dreadfully wrong, knowing that a splash from a beaver's big flat tail was normally a distress signal. I was relieved to learn that, in this case, it was just the beavers celebrating. They had managed to rebuild the dam. It was holding in the flowing water again. As soon as the good news reached the shore, many shouts of victory were heard in screeches, cries, grunts, stomping of feet, and any other means of expressing relief and joy. After the uproar had settled down somewhat, the animals began to stir themselves and chatter all in unison.

It wasn't until then that I realized that I ached all over from standing still for such a long period of time. The other creatures must have felt it too, for I saw many of them stretching and flexing unused muscles in an effort to get the kinks out. We animals were not used to remaining perfectly still for such a long period of time.

It was then, too, that I discovered how hungry I was. I had gone to bed dissatisfied that morning, and now it was

almost time for the sun to rise again. The other animals must have discovered the same thing, for we began to scatter immediately, knowing that we had little time to eat before another sunup.

I hurried off to the picnic site. It was disappointing. There were very few edibles in the barrels. It seemed that the rain had kept the barrels from being filled up as usual. I did manage to find a left-behind mouthful of apple core or soggy potato chip here and there upon the ground, but I soon gave up and knew that I must do my hunting elsewhere. I traveled the path to the meadow slowly, finding a cricket or some night crawlers here or there as I went.

When I reached the meadow, I found that the rain had affected it, too. All of the lower spots were little ponds. The tall grasses were no longer standing but seemed to be flat upon the ground, too tired to stand and hold the weight of water anymore.

Forest creatures stirred. Mrs. Deer and Cassandra were there. Cassandra called a greeting to me as soon as she spotted me. Mrs. Deer stopped feeding long enough to inquire about my home. I assured her that it would be fine once the creek waters had washed on by.

An owl swooped over our heads. He landed in a tree nearby and surveyed the world. It looked like his breakfast had been postponed too, because of the rains.

I moved on, poking at a stone here and an anthill there. Finally I decided to give up and go home. Home? I didn't even have my home. Where would I go until the creek gave me back my log? I remembered the fallen tree and the house of sorts under the branches and roots. I headed for it. It certainly wasn't comfortable like my home, but at least it was a place to hide away and sleep.

When I reached it, I checked it out carefully before I entered to make sure that no other animal had already occupied it. Then I went in and tried to make myself comfortable. There was no softness about the place. I didn't wonder that no other animal had chosen it. It didn't feel like home at all. I curled up in a tight, uncomfortable ball and told myself to go to sleep. Hopefully, by the next rising of the sun, I would be back in my own home where I belonged.

Chapter Fourteen

I was glad to leave my makeshift home that evening and shake loose some of my stiff muscles. My leafless bed did not suit me at all. I was hungry, too, and so I headed quickly for the pond. Here I found things back to normal. The beavers had done a good job on the dam and the danger of losing our much-needed water supply was past —at least for the present.

The frogs croaked, the raccoons dined, and the beavers and muskrats swam busily about. Nearby an owl hooted loudly. A fish left a silver arch as he dived into the air for a split second. I felt that my world had been restored to its proper order.

After having a refreshing drink, I left for the picnic area. I hoped that it was restored to proper order, too, and there was once again a large quantity of good things left behind by picnickers. During the rain, the pickings had been very scant indeed.

There was not an abundance of food in the barrels, but I did manage to find enough to satisfy my immediate needs. I started for the meadow thinking that I would add a few crickets and other tasty things to my menu before it was time for the sun's appearance.

The meadow too was filled with activity. Mrs. Deer and Cassandra were daintily picking their way across the shadowed side of the small area, feeding upon the grasses as they went. Three members of the rabbit family played tag or leapfrog—or perhaps it was a strange combination of the two. It seemed to have different rules from any game that I had ever watched before. They seemed to be enjoying it immensely. I stood and watched them for awhile. They called to me to come join them, but I knew better than to try. My legs would never work like theirs did.

When I moved on, looking for something edible as I made my way across the meadow, I was surprised by a squeaky voice calling my name. I looked up quickly and saw Cuddles approaching. I hastened to meet him, grinning as I did so.

"Hi, Cuddles."

"Hi, Fuzzle." He sounded out of breath.

"What brings you to the meadow?"

"Well," he squeaked, "I heard that the creek flooded again and you said that you lived down that way, so I came to see—"

"I'm fine. My log did get flooded though. I'm sleeping in a temporary place until it dries out again. I sure will be glad to get back home, though." Cuddles nodded as though he understood.

"Well," he said, "I'm glad that you are okay."

Our talk turned to other things then. I told Cuddles all about our pond and the beavers' fast work to fix the dam. He told me about the heavy rain and how it had concerned the animals in the pine forest. They had been worried that the storm might bring with it lightning that would start a forest fire. The forest was very dry because of a long spell without moisture. The neighborhood animals felt much safer now after the heavy rainfall and were actually very thankful for the rain that had almost flooded me out and threatened the life of all of the pond dwellers.

We were glad that no real harm had come with the storm; actually, the storm brought a lot of good. We took an ambling walk down to the pond to check things out. It was still higher than usual, but the beaver dam carefully regulated the flow of water now. The area of the pine forest was further down stream from the pond, so the animals who lived there could be assured of future water supply as well.

"I'd better be gettin'," said Cuddles in his squeaky voice. "I don't travel very fast and it is quite a ways back to my part of the forest."

"I sure do thank you for coming over. It's really been good to see you again," I assured him. "If I knew where to find you, I'd come over some night and visit you."

"Maybe some night we'll have time for me to come over and take you back. I'd love to show you my part of the woods and introduce you to my friends and family."

"Do you have a large family?" I asked him.

"No, not really. Not like the rabbits. It seems that no matter where you go in the woods, you find rabbits. We aren't too many in number, and we sort of scatter after we grow up. We don't get together very often, I'm afraid. I have a sister who lives not too far away and we see each other fairly frequently. She keeps in touch with my mother, who sees my oldest brother, who passes on word from my youngest brother. So we sort of keep in touch in a roundabout way."

I suddenly felt very sad. I didn't even have a sister nearby. And I had no idea where my mother was or any of the rest of my family. I allowed myself, for the first time in weeks, to wonder if I would ever find them again. I must be a long, long ways away from the woods where

I had been born.

Cuddles began to talk about when we could get together again, and the feeling of loneliness soon left me.

"I'm going to need to clean up my log house and get it dried out and re-lined with leaves and moss." I told him. "I hope that it won't be long until the water is gone and I am able to do that. After that I should be able to come almost anytime."

"Good," he squeaked, "I'll give you a few more days and then I'll look you up again."

"Great!" I said. "I'll see you then."

He left, and I headed back down the path toward my temporary home. We called to one another as we walked down the paths that led away from the pond in two different directions. Finally we were beyond calling distance.

I hadn't gone far when I met Flossie and Mittens Rabbit. They both were looking well-fed and plump. I didn't tell them so, but I thought that they actually were getting a little on the tubby side.

"Hi, Fuzzle," they said in unison, and then they both giggled. I didn't care much for giggling but I did answer them politely.

"Are you living over here now?" Mittens asked.

"Just for a few days." I replied.

"Then where are you going?" asked Flossie.

"Back home—to my log."

They both looked surprised at that and I wondered why but did not ask. Flossie changed the subject.

"Boy, did we have a good dinner tonight," she stated, patting her bulging sides. Mittens giggled again.

I felt like saying, "Yes, I noticed," but instead I asked, "Where?"

"Well," stated Flossie, rolling her eyes, "We aren't supposed to . . . Mama says . . . but we went to the garden patch of Mrs. Canning."

"Her name's not Canning, silly," squealed Mittens. "That's what she *does*. Her name's Peters."

The rabbits both laughed until I was fearful that their well-fed sides might pop. At last Mittens seemed to get control of herself.

"Do you like garden stuff?" she asked me.

"Oh, he prob'ly doesn't," cut in Flossie. "He likes crickets and frogs and things."

"Oh, but I do," I hastened to inform them. "I like many things. I remember visiting a garden with my family and we found all kinds of good things there. I especially like strawberries."

"Mrs. Peters doesn't have any strawberries," said Flossie.

"Mrs. Canning," teased Mittens, and they started to howl with laughter again. As soon as I felt that it was polite to do so I excused myself and said goodby, leaving them still rolling on the ground holding their shaking sides.

When I approached my makeshift abode, I told myself that I really should carry some moss and leaves to make things a bit softer; but I reminded myself that I might be back in my own bed very soon, so it would really be wasted effort. Besides, I was very tired from my long night of feeding and visiting. The sun would be up soon and I wanted nothing but to settle down and get some sleep, so I didn't bother. I crawled into the dark, damp hole beneath the fallen tree and curled up as comfortably as I could and was soon sound asleep.

Chapter Fifteen

The next night when I arose, I decided to go check on my old home even before I went to the pond. I was so anxious to get back into my own home again.

As I traveled down the path toward the area where my log lay on the creek bank, I met two of the rabbit family. They decided to join me and we headed for the log together. The squirrels heard us coming and, even though it was late in the day for them to be about, they went along. Even two of the younger coons joined our party and, just before we got there, a possum fell in with us, too.

I chatted nonstop the whole way, stating that as soon as possible I would clean out the log and put in dry material so that I could move in again. My constant talking did not stop my neighbors from talking as well, and we made quite a racket as we traveled down the woodland path together. A jay came out and scolded us soundly. She said that she had just settled her young down and our noisy exchange had wakened them all again. I mumbled my apology, but the jay was too busy scolding to even hear me. We did attempt to go more quietly after that though. Even the squirrels quieted down some.

By the time we reached the site of my log home, I was so excited I could hardly contain myself. I could see that the water had receded, and I hoped with all of my heart that the log would already be dry enough for me to start my clean-up job.

I ran forward eagerly and then stopped short. For a minute I was confused. My log was not where I had expected it to be. I must have become mixed up. I looked about me, trying to get my bearings and to decide if I should move to the left or the right. All of my animal friends stood around, too, straining their eyes and looking this way and that.

"That's funny," I finally said. "I thought that—"

"It's not here," cut in Skidder. "It's gone."

"What do you mean, it's gone? It's got to be around here—somewhere," I said lamely, stretching my neck and looking around as far as I could see.

"What are you looking for?" asked a kind voice above our heads. "Maybe I could help you."

We all looked up to see a very large owl on a limb above us.

"Fuzzle's log," spoke Skidder. "He had to leave it when the creek flooded and now it doesn't seem to be here."

"No," agreed the owl, "I'm afraid it isn't."

"Can you tell us where to find it then? Is it this way or that way?" I asked him hurriedly.

"Oh my, no!" said the owl. "It isn't this way or that way. It is gone."

"Gone?" many voices echoed together.

"Gone where?" I said weakly.

"Why it's gone the way it came," said Mr. Owl.

"The way it came?"

"Yes, on the water."

I was very puzzled, and began to wonder if the owl really knew anything at all about the situation.

"I don't think that I understand . . ."

"The log wasn't always there on the creek bank. It was not born and raised there," said the owl.

No one questioned him.

"No, indeed," he went on. "It came the way it left. With a flood."

"With a flood?"

I didn't want to believe it, but I thought that maybe I was beginning to understand after all.

"Yes, with a flood. Who knows where the log really came from. It was not there—and then, after a heavy rain and a flood, it was there. It laid there for many rains and many snows, and now with this flood it has moved on again."

"Where will I find it?" I asked and, even as I asked, I was afraid that the owl might not have the answer.

"You will not find it," he said with confidence. "It is now gone. Not even I know how far it has gone or where."

"But what will I do for a home?" As soon as I asked the question, the animal friends, who had been standing silently around me while I talked with the owl, burst forth with questions of their own. The noise was terrible. No one could hear or understand what the other person was asking. Nor if anyone was giving any answers. It was some time until the owl was able to restore order again. When he did, he said very simply, "You must find a new home."

We all wailed. Again he tried to restore order.

"Hush, hush," he said, "all of you. Why, I'm surprised at the fuss. You all know that there are many homes in the forest. The loss of one is no big problem. It happens all the time. We just move on and find a new home and fix it to suit our needs. You, Skidder. Have you always lived in the same home?"

"Well . . . no . . ." said Skidder.

"And you, Ringo," he asked one of the coons, "have you?"

"No, but—"

"And you, Mrs. Fluff?" he turned to a rabbit.

She only shook her head.

"You see," went on the owl. "There are homes aplenty in the forest. We just need to find one that we like and fix it up to suit ourselves."

I still didn't like it. I loved my log home, and I think that the other animals knew how I felt.

"But I—" I started.

"There's no need to fuss about it," said the owl. "One just needs to get busy at it."

There was silence for a moment, and then Skidder said, "We'll help," and a whole chorus of "we'll help" broke forth.

I appreciated their kindness.

"Thank you," I cried above the din. "Thank you, I appreciate it. I really do. But Skidder, it's already past your bedtime. And the rest of you, it's time for breakfast. I think that we should all go about our usual ways and keep an eye open for what might make a suitable home. Then we can meet at the pond just before sunup and see if anyone has found anything. If not, then I will sleep in my temporary home again and we'll try again tomorrow night. If in the meantime, Skidder sees anything during the time of the sun, he can let us know."

"That's very good thinking," said the owl, and I felt very grownup and smart.

After much calling and talking and chattering, we made a noisy departure, promising to meet at the pond just before daylight. I walked toward the picnic area and the raccoons joined me.

Ringo made an effort to cheer me up. "With all of us looking," he said, "we'll have you a new home in no time. And I bet that you'll like it even better than the other one."

I hoped sincerely that he was right, but I will admit that I was just a bit dubious.

Chapter Sixteen

It was getting on toward sunrise when I hurried to the pond to meet my friends. I had watched carefully as I traveled through the woods that night, but I had found nothing that looked like a suitable home for me. I hoped that one of my friends might have been more successful.

When I approached the pond I saw that many of them had already gathered. They were talking excitedly in a babble of voices. I hurried forward expecting each of them to have two or three places to show me. That was not the case. As I drew near, the chattering subsided completely and everyone seemed to wait for someone else to begin.

"Well," I said expectantly, "where do we start?"

There was no answer.

"Didn't anyone find something suitable?" I said slowly. They only shook their heads. "Nor did I." I shook my head also and I must have sounded very sad. Still no one spoke.

I turned to go back down the path when a deep voice above me said almost reproachfully, "Why so glum?

There is plenty of time. You have only searched for one night. There are plenty of homes about. The proper one will be found at the proper time.'' It was the owl.

I picked up my drooping tail and gave it a smart fluff. Of course he was right. I turned back to my friends.

''Well, we'll keep looking. There are plenty of good homes here in the forest. We'll find just the right one.''

A general noise of chatter followed my statement.

''And now,'' I continued, ''we'd better all be off to bed before that sun gets too high in the sky and the day folk think that we have decided to take over the day as well as the night.''

The forest creatures laughed at my poor attempt at humor. Even though my joke had not been a good one, the effect of the laughter was good on us all and we went off to our beds in a much better mood.

I did not sleep well in my temporary shelter. It was not at all to my liking. I kept thinking about not finding anything better and having to spend the rest of my life in the place. Well, I finally decided, if I did, I did. I would just make an effort to fix it up and make it as comfortable as possible, and it would do. I wasn't happy with that thought but it was an improvement over fretting over something that I could do nothing about.

That evening I crawled from my hard bed and set out for the pond. The first order of the night would be to care for my tummy. After my drink I was ready to head for the picnic barrels. The picnic sight was already a buzz of activity. People called to me to ask me if I had heard of anything yet, and I answered that I hadn't but I was sure that something would turn up soon.

The barrels were not yielding as many good things as they had been earlier in the summer, and most of us left the area still hungry and had to move on to see what else we could find.

I met Mittens and Flossie and they told me that I was welcome to come with them to Mrs. Peters' garden patch. Mrs. Peters was always in bed when they arrived, being a day creature rather than a night creature. They also cautioned that she had a dog and he didn't seem to have too much preference to day or night and would set up barking at any time if he was disturbed. They were confident that they could raid the garden without him sending forth an alarm.

It sounded good and I was hungry. I remembered well the round sides of the rabbits after a visit to the garden, so I thanked them for their invitation and fell in beside them.

It was a bit of a walk to the Peters'. I was sure that the rabbits would have been able to cover the ground much more quickly had they not been setting the pace for me. I wondered if they were annoyed at my slowness but they said nothing to indicate that they were. Rabbits, I decided, are very polite and patient people.

When we did arrive, at last, at the Peters', I found it just as the rabbits had said. The fenced-in garden was full of tasty things to eat. Some of the food had already been harvested by the humans but there was still plenty that had been left behind.

I nosed about, trying a bit of this and a taste of that. Most of it was delicious, though I did find one or two things that I decided I would leave for the rabbits. They were not to my liking.

We ate our fill and each grabbed another mouthful as we left the patch. This we chewed as we waddled down the path toward the woods. We were greedy and full and wanting to just crawl in somewhere and go to sleep. Even the rabbits were not anxious to travel fast, as their sides bulged every bit as much as my own did.

I thought that we would never reach the pond, but even-

tually we did. Our friends were waiting for us, a bit impatiently I'm afraid. It was then that I realized that, in my preoccupation of eating all that I could hold, I had not even thought to watch for a good future home. I blushed as the thought passed through my mind. How could I expect my friends to remember if even *I* had forgotten?

The reports on this night were not too encouraging. A few had suggestions about something that they had spotted, but always there was someone else who had also seen the potential home and declared it to not be suitable at all. We were about ready to leave when Skidder came bounding in.

"Hey," he called, "did you find anything?"

We all answered in unison that nothing had been found.

Skidder skidded to a halt. He was panting from his run.

"I saw a fallen tree," he said. "It might work out just fine." And he began to describe it to me. He hadn't gone far when I realized that he was describing my present abode. I smiled at him.

"Yeah," I said, "I saw it, too. In fact, that's where I am living right now."

Skidder looked a little embarrassed and I didn't want him to be, so I hurried on, "And if I don't find anything else, it will work just fine. I'll just fix the bed up, seal off the north a bit better, and it'll . . ."

I didn't finish. I still didn't like the location.

We all decided to go home to bed and try again the next night. We had just turned down the path when Cassandra and Mrs. Deer approached. They were both very shy and rarely sought out the other animals for visiting, though they were the most polite animals in the forest. When they came to join us now, a tingle of excitement ran through the whole group.

"We hear that you are looking for a home, Fuzzle," said Mrs. Deer.

"That's right," I answered very softly, for no one spoke roughly or loudly to Mrs. Deer.

"Cassandra thinks that she might have found something. You tell him, dear," and she gently nudged Cassandra forward.

Excitement filled Cassandra's voice.

"It's over near our meadow," she said. "It's a log, much like you had before, only a bit bigger, I think. It's dry and in a place where it should never be reached by flood waters. It's almost hidden, so it should be private." Privacy was very important to the deer family. "It is close to the meadow and not far from the pond or the picnic area," she continued.

I felt about ready to burst.

"Can we see it?" I asked and almost forgot to be polite. "Could you show us?"

"Of course," she answered and turned to lead the way.

We all followed her. The other animals of the forest seemed just as excited as I over the possibility of a new home. We tried to be gentle and mannerly as we hurried after the deer, but there was some chattering and skipping, I'm afraid.

When we reached the site, Cassandra had to take us right up to the log, it was so hidden. I don't think that any of us would have spotted it on our own. I wondered how she had ever found it.

The entrance, though partly concealed, was wide and allowed plenty of room for passage. Even I, with my bulging sides, had no difficulty in passing through comfortably. Inside it was perfect. Way toward the back was a perfect sleeping room. It was soft with the dust of the rotting log, and with a little moss and some dry leaves would be cozy and warm. I ached to just curl up in it on the spot and claim it for my home.

"Jiminy whiz!" I said, grinning as I looked around.

I went back out to tell Cassandra that it was just what I had been looking for. As soon as I came out, my friends took turns going in to check over the new home. They were as excited as I was, and each of them in turn told me it was quite the nicest skunk home that they had ever been in.

I thanked Cassandra the best that I could. I knew that I would never be able to really tell her how much I appreciated the home that she had found for me.

She hung her head shyly, but she gave me a delightful smile.

The clattering and chattering around me made me aware of my other friends.

"How do you want it fixed?"

"What do you need?"

"Let's do it now."

"What shall we bring?"

Everyone was talking at once, and I knew that they wouldn't be happy until I was properly settled. I tried to force my sleepy eyes to stay open for a bit longer so that I could respond to my friends.

"I use moss and leaves," I answered them. Animals scurried off in many directions.

Skidder was soon back with a mouthful of soft dry moss.

"You go in and we'll bring you the material and you can arrange it just the way you want it," he told me.

I went in and put Skidder's moss just where I wanted it.

The leaves and moss came, load after load. I pushed and poked and arranged it—just where I wanted it—and still it kept coming. I poked in some more and tucked a bit more about my feet and then pushed a bit more in at the head and padded my bed a bit. It looked so inviting that I could hardly keep myself from crawling into it. I went out to hold the supply line and inform my friends that I had all of the material that I could use. The birds had gathered around my door. Even the jays had joined

them and, instead of scolding as they usually did, they were the spokesmen.

"The softness of a bed is in the feathers," said Mrs. Jay, presenting a feather to me in her beak. I hardly knew what to say. I had never slept on a feather bed before.

"If you'd like to come out," said Mrs. Finch in a quiet voice, "we'll just go in and arrange them."

I stepped out. One by one the birds took their turn, going in with a feather held in the mouth and returning in a flash with nothing but a contented smile. I knew that they were proud to be able to make my bed properly.

"There now," said Mrs. Sparrow, the last one to deposit her feather; and I knew that she was satisfied that my bed was ready for occupancy.

"Thank you—thank you all. For the moss and the leaves . . . and the feathers. And thank you, Cassandra, for the home. I'm sure that I will be very happy here. I can hardly wait to try it."

That was so true. The sun was now shining down on the earth, warming us all and making us night creatures even drowsier. I knew that my friends were all tired, and I appreciated the fact that they had stayed up so long in order to help me get moved in.

"And now," I said, "I'm going to go and test it out."

They left, by two's and three's, hurrying down the various paths toward their own homes; and I crawled into my new home and went to my new bed. The softness of it was like being on a cloud. I wondered why we skunks had never made our beds with feathers before. It was absolutely delightful. I curled up as tightly as my still-full tummy would allow and let my body sink deeply into the softness of my bed and then went to sleep. And such a sleep I had. I had never been more comfortable or slept more soundly. I promised myself that I would be sure to tell all of my woodland friends that never could there be a softer bed or a more delightful home than mine.

Chapter Seventeen

When I awoke that night, I felt great. My full tummy had made me contented and my soft bed had given me a good rest. I climbed out of my bed, almost hating to leave its comfort, but I told myself that it was something to look forward to coming back to and finally talked myself into venturing forth.

Some of my friends were waiting at my door when I made my appearance. They wanted to know just how I had liked my bed. I assured them that I had never slept better and from the way that I looked and grinned, I'm sure that they believed me.

We headed to the pond together. There was a coolness in the air. I had felt it approaching for some time now and each night it seemed to be just a bit sharper.

Other animals seemed to notice it too. Without saying so, we hurried a bit with our breakfast gathering. I think that all of us were thinking about getting back to our beds as quickly as possible.

Again the picnic area did not yield much in the way of a meal. I went with the rabbits to Mrs. Peters' garden patch again. I noticed that one of the coons was also there, but after a curt greeting he took himself to the far side of the garden and seemed to suggest that he would be happy if we'd stay on our side. We did. There was plenty for everyone, so there was no need to argue about it.

We ate quickly and headed for home with full tummies again. As we walked off down the path, I heard the dog begin to bark. Another animal must have come into the patch that wasn't as cautious and careful as we had been, and the guard dog had been aroused from his sleep.

I was glad that we had finished and were on our way home. The barking dog was no threat to us.

We walked slowly and when we reached the dividing of our ways, I bid the rabbits good night and headed gladly for my bed. It was so good to enter into my own home and crawl deeply into the warmth and snugness of my bed. Again I slept well, thankful for the friends who had provided me with my comfort.

The days and nights proceeded much the same in the weeks that followed. I slept throughout the day and hunted where my path led me at night. Mrs. Peters cleaned out her garden, and there was very little left after she was through. It did appear that she was determined to carefully bundle everything away for the winter. The weather was getting colder and colder. On more than one morning the grass was frosted as I headed back for my log. I noticed changes in my friends as well. A number of them had thickened their coats and the rabbits were changing theirs from the summer brown to the winter white. The squirrels were busy from sunup to sundown, it seemed. I could often hear them as they scurried back and forth with seeds and nuts in their mouths. When I asked Skidder what they were up to, he answered without even stopping,

"Storing—for winter."

The deer moved deeper into the woods, so I did not see Cassandra or her mother. I thought of going looking for Cuddles. We still hadn't gotten together for our trip into his woods. He had sent a message with a flicker one day that he thought it best to wait for spring. I agreed. I did not want to be out at night any longer than was absolutely necessary.

As the days passed and the air grew colder, a desire to just curl up and sleep and sleep began to overtake me. As long as there was food around, I felt that I should stir myself and go and eat something. But I knew with each new night that I would not be able to talk myself into venturing forth much longer. The food was getting more and more scarce, and my body was more and more inclined to just bury itself in my soft bed and forget the whole thing.

I talked to the rabbits about it one night on my way back from a trip to the almost-empty garden.

"Do you feel like you just want to go to bed and sleep and sleep?" I asked them.

"No, why? Do you?"

"I sure do," I told them. "I can hardly get myself to stir anymore."

"Then do it," they stated simply.

"But I haven't stored," I told them. "Skidder has been busy for weeks."

They looked at my chubby sides.

"You've stored," they assured me.

I looked down at my roundness and knew that they were right. I began to laugh.

"I guess you're right. I have stored, haven't I?"

We walked on together.

"Do you store?" I asked them.

They shook their heads.

"No need," they said. "There is plenty of food for us throughout the whole winter. We eat bark and such when there are no gardens."

"Am I the only one who just sleeps?" I hoped that I wasn't *that* different from the other animals.

"Oh, no," they hastened to inform me. "A number of the animals sleep—all winter long."

I felt a little better then. At least it wasn't just laziness on my part.

When we reached the place where the path divided, I stopped for a moment.

"You know," I said, "I think that I will just do that."

"Do what?" asked Mr. G. Rabbit.

"Sleep. Just go to bed and sleep and sleep."

"It's likely time all right," said Mrs. T. Rabbit.

"Oh, yes, it's time. Some of the animals have already gone to bed. It's pretty cold now."

"How will I know when to wake up?" I asked, rather alarmed at the thought that I might just go right on sleeping.

"You'll know."

"No problem. They always know."

"I'm not sure what wakens them, but they always know."

"Spring—when spring comes you'll know it's time to wake up."

With all of their assurances ringing in my ears, I was more relaxed about going to bed.

"Well," I said, "I guess I'll see you in the spring then. I hope that you all have a good winter."

I looked about me at the group of rabbit friends who had gathered around my door. They were all dressed in heavy warm white coats. They did not look sleepy like I

felt, nor did they look concerned about the coming winter. They looked quite content with themselves.

"We'll see you in the spring," they answered me and then they left to go off toward their own homes.

I turned into the log home that I called mine. Snow was falling now, drifting down softly. I thought of the feathers that lined my nest. The snow looked just as light and soft as those feathers felt. I watched it for a few minutes and then I went to bed. I was so sleepy. What I needed was a good long sleep. I curled up tightly and allowed my eyes to drift shut. I smiled to myself in the darkness. My bed felt so good. I would just stay right where I was. I'd see the world and the woods, the meadow and the pond—I'd see it all again in the spring.

Chapter Eighteen

Over the next weeks, I vaguely remember stirring a few times, but each time I would just turn over and go to sleep again. Actually, it seemed that it was really a very short while until I found myself feeling the urge to move from my warm bed. I arose, rather stiffly, stretched and yawned, stretched and turned, and stretched some more. My muscles that hadn't been used for some weeks were still there, even though they didn't seem to work quite as well as they had when I put them to bed.

I sniffed the air. There was something different about it. It smelled fresh and clear, and an excitement passed through me. Carefully and slowly I began to move forward.

When I reached my doorway, the world seemed full of activity. Bird-song greeted me and animals scurried back and forth. To my surprise it was still broad daylight, and not being a day person, I turned reluctantly to go back to my bed. It was difficult to do. I was eager to get out and find my friends and hear all of the news of the winter. Besides, I now was aware of my empty stomach. Oh, how hungry I was! I looked down at myself and found that, over the winter of sleep, I had lost my well-rounded look.

I tried to curl up and go back to sleep, but my stomach insisted that it must have something to fill it—and soon. Eventually, I gave up and crawled from my bed again. If I went carefully, surely it would be okay for me to seek my breakfast in the daytime—just this once.

I went to the door of my home and peered out. The bright sunlight hurt my eyes, and I had to stand for some time to adjust to it. At last I felt that I would be able to see well enough to travel to the pond and headed in that direction.

Snow still lay in sheltered places, and little trickles of water ran or dripped here and there. Tiny bits of green were showing through in some of the sun-splashed spots. I could hear the chattering of the jays. I wondered if their quarrels had continued all winter long. A few songs mingled with the chatter. They came from the song sparrows and chickadees. The robins and bluebirds were not yet back from their trip to the South.

The first person that I saw as I hurried down the path was Skidder. He looked like he had put on weight, rather than lost it, over the winter. He was still running with a nut in his mouth—just as I had last seen him in the fall. When he saw me, he dropped it and called out.

"Hi, Fuzzle. How was your winter?"

I hurried to meet him.

"Fine. I slept like a top in my feather bed. And how was yours?"

"It was a long, hard winter," he said seriously. "It didn't bother me any because I had plenty stored away, but it was hard on some of the animals. I'm sure that they will be glad for the warmer weather and better food supply."

I was surprised to hear of the winter. It was so easy for me to forget that it had even been.

"Who had problems?" I asked, concerned about my friends.

"The rabbits found it especially hard. Many of them look really thin. They should start picking up now. I saw a little green grass this morning. That is good news to the rabbits."

I was sorry to hear about my rabbit friends. I remembered how some of them had generously shared their garden patch with me in the fall.

"It was hard for the birds, too, but the Peters put out feeders for them and this helped them tremendously. I don't know how they would have made it without the help of the humans."

Skidder changed his tone. "But spring is here now and we all will be getting fat and saucy again."

I didn't tell him that I thought he looked plenty fat and saucy as he was.

Suddenly he stopped short.

"What are you doing up?"

I stopped, too.

"It's spring," I said simply.

"But I mean in the daytime. Did you decide over the winter to become a day creature?"

"No," I laughed. "I'm just so hungry that I decided to see what I could find."

"I'm afraid that there won't be much yet. No berries, no picnic barrels, not many bugs . . . a few frogs."

"Frogs!" I said in disgust, remembering my poor attempts at catching them.

When we reached the pond, I was surprised to see that it still had ice covering parts of it. A small section was free and flowing where the beavers had kept it open. There were not many people around that I knew. The other night creatures were smarter than I and were waiting for night to fall before going out to look for their breakfast.

I was terribly hungry, but Skidder had been right. There wasn't much to eat. I pushed around at logs and rocks and did stir a few small things. It seemed that the few bits that I found only made my stomach feel worse. At last I decided to go back to bed and wait until dark like I was supposed to. I crawled into my bed and fluffed my warm feathers about me. Then I curled up tightly and managed to go back to sleep.

It was several days later that I crawled from my bed again. I had had no idea when I went back to sleep that I would not wake up again as soon as it was dark . . . but I didn't.

When I came out from my log, the sun was just going down. The air was still chilly but the smell of fresh growing things was all about me.

I stood still and sniffed—first this way and then that—it all smelled so good.

Again I headed for the pond. This time I met two of the rabbit family on the trail. Skidder had been right. They were still thin, though they assured me that they had had some very good eating in the past few days. They seemed very pleased with themselves—and with the springtime. Their coats were busy changing back to the soft summer brown.

I left them after our brief chat and went on to Lookingglass Pond. I could hear the croaking of the frogs before I even got to the last bend in the trail. There was splashing too, and I knew that other animals were already there before me.

There were two raccoons. One was busily washing his breakfast and the other was crouching very still by the water's edge. I knew that he was frog-hunting, and so I stood where I was so as not to spoil his chances. Soon there was a quick movement and his hand came up from the water holding his dinner.

My empty stomach churned within me. Oh, how I envied him his catch. I decided to try it. I knew that my hunger would make me impatient, but I had to try. There just wasn't much food around this early in the year.

I positioned myself as close to the water as I dared and waited with held breath. Not a thing stirred about me. I thought that I had surely picked a very bad spot and one totally uninhabited and was about to move on in disgust, when my eye caught a slight movement. There near to me was a pair of big eyes. I knew that the frog was beyond my reach and my only hope was to wait for him to move closer. I set myself to waiting. My stiff muscles complained and my stomach growled. Surely, I thought, I could stand it no longer. Just when I was about to give up and leave the cold water of the pond, another frog came swimming toward the other. He was a big fellow and seemed to be out to prove a point. In fact, it appeared that he himself had decided that the smaller frog might make *him* a meal. I watched him approach—not moving, every muscle tense—and just as he was ready to strike—I struck instead. I could hardly believe my eyes. I got him! The littler fellow gave a surprised and then happy croak and splashed away.

The rest of the night I spent foraging, finding little bits of food wherever I could. It was slow and plodding work, and when the night was over I was far from satisfied as I went back to my bed.

The next several nights went the same way, and then a strange thing happened. It began to snow again. I was bewildered and frustrated by it all. It seemed that the spring had not been of very long duration. And where had the summer and fall gone? I hadn't even noticed them come and go.

I headed back to my log den, shaking my head at the

mixed-up world as I went. On the way I met Flossie. Mittens was not with her.

"Where are you going?" Flossie asked me. "It's not time for the sun yet."

"I'm going home," I said disgustedly. "It's snowing again. Doesn't seem to me that it should be time for winter again already. Why I haven't had one decent meal yet and here it's time—"

Flossie began to laugh.

"Grandfather says that it might snow a number of times before summer is here. It has already snowed and thawed many times this spring. You just missed them because you were still sleeping; that's all. The sun will likely melt it all first thing in the morning."

"You really think so?"

"Sure . . . just you wait and see."

I felt better about what Flossie said, but I went on to bed anyway. I slept for several days before I wakened and came out again. Flossie was right about one thing. The sun had melted the snow. It was cool in the night air, but I could tell that things had been much warmer during the day. I could see patches of green all around me now, and when I met Flossie she looked like she was losing her lean, shaggy look of winter. I missed Mittens again and asked Flossie about her.

"Oh, she lives over near the meadow now and doesn't come out too far from home right now. She had a family of her own, you know."

I was surprised at the news but I guess that I shouldn't have been.

"That's very nice," I said and Flossie grinned in agreement.

After finding what I could to eat I went back to bed again. I would be so glad when there was again more food available. I never was going to get over my skinniness on my present rations.

Several nights passed, and it seemed that all I was able to do was to find little scraps here and there. However, I did realize that each night it improved somewhat, and I began to have hope that soon there would be enough food to actually fill me up.

Cuddles came to see me. I was good to see him again. His voice was still squeaky and his coat full of his sharp needles, but he didn't look as though the winter had been hard on him at all. He kidded me a bit.

"My goodness, Fuzzle, what you lost in weight you sure made up for in height. Look at you. You've almost doubled your size."

I hadn't thought of it until he mentioned it, but I suddenly realized that he was right. I had grown. Why, I bet that I was almost as tall as my mother. I did wish that I could see her again just to show off a bit. I wondered what she would think of her near-grown son. I grinned a bit and was glad that Cuddles had noticed.

Cuddles was anxious to show me his part of the woods, so we started off as soon as I had eaten a few bites.

It was a long walk for two creatures who didn't walk very fast. No wonder Cuddles didn't visit often.

The woods were different where he lived. There were many pines and spruces scattered among the trees. The creatures who lived there were either shy or unfriendly, it seemed, and so we didn't stop to chat much. Cuddles knew some of them by name and called out greetings when we met. They answered politely enough but sort of moved out of our way to let us pass.

Cuddles loved his part of the forest. It was evident as he showed me around. He pointed out objects of interest and excitedly told me about them in his squeaky voice. I enjoyed his tour to such an extent that I forgot to watch the changing sky. Suddenly, we both realized that the night would soon be over and it was a long way back to Wonder Meadow.

I told Cuddles that he needn't come with me, that it would make him too late getting back to his area again. I bid him a hasty goodby, with a promise to see him again, and headed for my home in a lopsided lope. I knew that before I arrived I would witness another sunrise. I must learn to keep an eye on our moon-clock.

Chapter Nineteen

The weeks passed quickly. Each day brought more sunshine and more green things. The air had a definite feeling of warmth. The robins began to appear, as well as the crows, the ducks, the bluebirds, and all manner of spring birds. Mothers came from their winter dens with wobbly new youngsters following along behind them. Some babies were already several weeks old and were now taken out on expeditions. Others were quite young but took easily to the ways of the woods. Baby rabbits seemed to be everywhere, at various ages and stages of development. I didn't suppose that there was a prouder mother in the entire woods than was Mittens. She brought her first litter over to see me. They were a very cuddly bunch and as she introduced them—three girls and two boys—they nodded their heads shyly and then ducked behind their mother or one another.

It wasn't long until the first picnickers arrived. They didn't fill the barrels with their good things, but what they did leave behind brought cries of joy from those of us who visited the site. We were anxious for more of their friends to join them.

My sides soon began to fill out again. In fact, I was beginning to look quite handsome. I was tall and firm, my coat was silky and shiny, and I made sure that I groomed it carefully each day. One never knew just whom one might meet in the forest!

I should have been completely happy. The night air was pleasant, there was once again a good food supply, the small creek bubbled contentedly as it flowed to the beaver-dam controlled pond, and my friends all called to me and chatted whenever we met. I was well liked and lived in a good land. I loved Pleasant Woods, Wonder Meadow, Looking-glass Pond, and especially my log home. But for some reason that I could not name there was a deep restlessness within me.

I decided to do more traveling. When night came I would hurry to the pond and get a drink, greeting those whom I met hurriedly, not even stopping to chat; then I was off to the picnic area for my meal. Seldom were we ever disappointed now. There were picnickers who used the area almost every day. Should there not be food there, there was plenty in the forest or the meadow. It just took a little longer to find, that was all.

After I had breakfasted, I hurried off on my own, wandering wherever the night wind drew me.

One night my venture took me across the meadow and to a field beyond. I was hurrying along, hardly mindful of where I was going, my mind on other things, when I looked up and saw a young deer just beyond me. I murmured a polite "hello" and started again on my way when the soft calling of my name stopped me.

I looked more closely then. It came to my mind that something about that graceful, young doe should be familiar to me.

"Don't you recognize me?" she asked gently, and at

that very moment I did. It was Cassandra. She was beautiful! She was almost as tall as her mother and she moved with a grace and beauty that was outstanding, even for a deer.

"You're lovely," I said with awe in my voice, then feeling silly, I hurried on. "I mean . . . I mean you've grown up. Why you're almost full grown. How are you . . . and how is your mother?"

She laughed softly, "Why thank you, Fuzzle. You have grown up yourself. I hardly recognized you. Just look at you!"

I blushed a bit. Cassandra went on. "Mother is fine. She is feeding over on the other side of that knoll with the herd. There are other deer in the forest, too." This time Cassandra blushed, and I wondered just who those other deer were and what they meant to Cassandra.

"A beau?" I inquired in a teasing voice, but Cassandra just laughed a soft, silvery laugh that made her even more beautiful.

"I must go," she said. "Mother will be wondering about me. It's been good to see you, Fuzzle."

We said goodby and Cassandra moved off gracefully. I watched her, trying to understand all of the changes that had come to us both over the months.

I had been seeing changes all around me and yet they had not really been registering, I'm afraid. All of us—Cassandra, Mittens, Flossie, me, and I'm sure many other young of the woods—had been growing up in those months. Perhaps that was why I was feeling so restless. Perhaps it was a part of growing up.

I moved on again. I was still searching—for what I wasn't sure. Adventure maybe . . . or excitement . . . for my family. Suddenly it became very important to me that I seemed to be the only skunk in the forest. That's what I was searching for! More of my kind. I was lonely, even though I was among friends.

I moved forward eagerly. Now that I knew just what it was that I was looking for, it should be much easier to find.

I didn't find a fellow skunk though and soon realized that it was time for me to head for home and go to sleep for the day.

That night I hurriedly ate and drank and headed out in another direction. Night after night I continued looking and hoping. Finally I would give up and head back for my bed, discouraged and frustrated. There just weren't any other skunks in our woods. Perhaps I would need to move on—leave behind the pond, the meadow, the picnic area, the woods, my log home, and all of my friends—and travel to a new woods where I could find some of my own kind. I hated the thought of it and I told no one of my thinking, but day by day the idea grew.

I went to see Cuddles. Perhaps, I thought, he has seen skunks in his area of the woods. I had difficulty in finding him. When I did, he greeted me joyfully, squeakily, and came down from his tree.

"Didn't expect to be seeing you," he told me. "Thought that you would be far too busy enjoying all of the good things to eat."

I patted my full round sides and grinned at Cuddles.

"Oh, I have been doing that," I assured him, "but a body can't spend all of his time eating."

Cuddles squeaked a funny little laugh. "I could," he said. "Takes me a long time to get filled up, and then it's time to start over again."

We chatted a while before I got up the courage to ask Cuddles what I had come to ask him.

"Have you ever seen any skunks around here, Cuddles?" I tried not to let it seem too important.

Cuddles came back quickly, "Why? Is one bothering

you, trying to come into your territory?''

Animals are very concerned about their territory and I instantly corrected Cuddles in his thinking.

''Oh, no. No, nothing like that. I just seems that I'm the only skunk in the whole area and I . . . well . . . I'd be glad to *share* my territory. I'd like to know some of my own kind, Cuddles. Why, I don't even know where my family is. I've never even seen another skunk to talk to since the day that I left home—and I didn't leave home willingly either.''

Cuddles thought deeply for a few minutes.

''No,'' he said, ''I guess I never have. Never gave it much thought before, but I guess maybe you are the only skunk hereabouts.''

We talked briefly about other things, and then I headed for home and let Cuddles go back to his eating.

All the way home I thought of my problem. It did look like I would need to leave Pleasant Woods.

I crawled into my bed and curled up. How I hated the thought of leaving my nice warm home. Would I ever find friends again who would be as good to me? Would I ever find a place to live that would be so ideal? Was it really that important to live among one's own kind that I should leave all that I had in order to try to find another skunk? Maybe not. I'd need to give it more thought the next evening. At least if I did go, I should give it very careful consideration first. I put aside my problem and went to sleep.

Chapter Twenty

The next evening I crawled from my bed, stretched to ease my muscles, and trotted from my log. I sniffed deeply of the clean fresh air around me. I loved my home and all that surrounded it. I decided that I would enjoy it to the full.

On the path I met Flossie and her new family. She kept an eye on her offspring as we chatted about the neighborhood news. I didn't hurry off as I had been doing of late, but took plenty of time for a good visit.

When I did finally move on to the pond, I spent time there as well. The large raccoon, Congo, was busy fishing, and this took even more time and patience than hunting frogs. I waited silently as I watched him. I did not want to frighten away his breakfast. At last he flipped a rather small sized fish to the bank, and I moved forward for a drink. He gave me a nod in appreciation and took his breakfast elsewhere to eat.

I spent a few minutes visiting with the beavers. Joe and Mrs. Joe were proudly showing off their two new babies. The babies could already swim like they had been born in the water—which indeed they had. I smiled and called words of praise for the youngsters and finally decided that I should be on my way.

When I got to the picnic area there was plenty of activity. A possum stood balancing on the edge of one of the barrels while he rummaged around in its interior, looking for the choicest morsels. Mrs. Black Bear was back. Two new cubs trotted at her heels and tumbled and wrestled whenever she took her eyes off of them. It was clear that they weren't too concerned with where their next meal was coming from. A rather small coon that I had not met before was sniffing under the table, and by the sounds of his pleased grunts, he was having success in finding something to his liking.

I moved slowly into the clearing, and the mother bear called her cubs to her side. She did not leave the clearing but made sure that her wayward cubs stayed nearby.

I moved over to a vacated barrel and began to pick and choose what I would have for breakfast. It was nice to have a choice.

"If I move away," I reminded myself, "I may not have a picnic area nearby." I had heard other animals speak of the added advantage that the picnic area had brought to the community. Hunting for food had not always been this easy. I soon had eaten all that I wanted, and the night was still young. I decided to take a walk and see the meadow before retiring. I hoped that some of my friends might be there.

As I walked, I still thought of my problem. If only I knew what to do. I was walking along deep in thought when a deep voice above me said, "Good evening."

I looked up. There sat Mr. Owl on a limb above my head.

"Good evening," I replied. "I'm sorry. I didn't see you."

"I noticed," said the owl, "you seemed to be a million miles away. Something on your mind?"

I smiled. "Well, yes. I'm afraid there is."

When I didn't go on, the owl spoke again. "Anything that I could help you with?"

"I'm not sure . . . it's just . . . well . . ." I hardly knew how to express myself. "Well . . . I've been thinking. You're not the only owl in the forest, are you?"

"No, but what—"

"And there are a number of deer, and several beavers, and many rabbits and even more than one possum and raccoon; and I've seen ever so many squirrels, even though they are day people and I'm a night person . . . and—"

"Hey," said Mr. Owl, "slow down a bit. I don't think that I'm following."

"Well . . . it's just . . . all of these animals have family, and well . . . have you ever seen another skunk in this forest?"

"I see," said the owl. "I see." He sat for a moment in silence. "You are right. I don't believe that I have ever seen another skunk in our forest. I had never thought of it . . ."

"Well, I have," I said rather sharply. "I think of it all the time. Do you know what it is like to be all alone? I mean without any of your kind around?"

"Rather lonely, I would imagine."

"It sure is. And well . . . I just don't know what to do about it."

"Do?" asked the owl, "What do you mean? What can you *do* about it?"

"I'm not sure. I've been trying to figure it out. I can stay here and be all alone, or I could move to another area and maybe find some of my own kind."

"I see," the owl blinked his eyes. "We'd hate for you to move away, Fuzzle."

"So would I," I said and as I spoke the words, I knew just how much I meant them.

"So," asked the owl, "what are your plans?"

"I don't know. I just don't know. I would hate to leave here. I love it here with all of my friends; but, boy, it sure does get lonely."

"You do have a real problem," the owl said.

"What do *you* think I should do?" I asked him, hoping for wisdom beyond my own.

"Well, that's a very tough decision to make."

I could tell that he was thinking about it, so I waited patiently. He clicked his beak and blinked his eyes and thought very seriously. Finally he spoke.

"I think," he said, "that you should not be hasty. Such a decision as moving from one's home should not be made lightly. It will take careful consideration. You should take at least seven moons to think about it and then do what you think is best. In the meantime, you should enjoy your friends of the forest and the home that you have."

I grinned.

"That's about what I decided on my own," I told the owl.

"Then you are a very wise skunk," the owl informed me. "You already had your answer and I think it was a good one."

"Well, I didn't really," I corrected him. "I hadn't really thought it through so well, I was just . . . well, I was sort of *acting* it through.

"That's good," said the owl. "Our thoughts should result in actions."

Another owl hooted across the woods, and the owl smiled.

"I must go," he said. "Mrs. Owl is calling. My, oh, my. I'm not sure, Fuzzle, if you really should become a family man or not. It takes Mrs. Owl and me our entire time just to try to fill the mouths of our hungry youngsters.''

With a chuckle he left me and I hurried on down the path toward the meadow. Mr. Owl was right. I would think seriously before I moved away. I could endure the loneliness for another seven moons.

I had reached the meadow and was investigating a rotten log, when a movement nearby caught my attention. I looked up quickly and moved back silently into the shadows. My eyes pierced into the dimness of the night, and I saw the meadow grasses waving slightly as an animal moved gently through them. Then to my utter astonishment and joy, a skunk stepped forward into the light of the moon! I stood as one transfixed, unable to believe my eyes!

When at last I convinced myself that I truly was not seeing things, I moved forward, holding myself in check lest I approach too eagerly.

''Hi,'' I said, and the excitement must have shown in my voice.

''Hello,'' she spoke hesitantly, shyly.

''You're new here aren't you?''

''Am I in your territory?'' she questioned, apology showing in her voice.

''Oh, no. I mean, well, yes. But I don't mind. I mean I've been wishing that . . .'' I didn't know how to say it and I felt so dumb. ''What I mean is . . . there's plenty of territory here for more than one.''

''Really?''

''Really,'' I hurried on, ''Where are you from? I mean, will you be able to stay or does your family . . .?''

''My family lives way across the field and over the hill. There are too many of us for the area now, and Mother told us that it was time for us to be on our own—to find our own territory—but she warned us not to encroach on someone else's, so if I'm—''

"Oh, no, no. Why, there's lots here and I'm all alone. I'd love to share—really."

The thought of her moving on again, without my even having a chance to get acquainted, frightened me. "Really," I said again. "Please, I'd love to have you stay."

"Well," she said slowly, "if you are sure."

"I'm sure. Really I'm sure!"

I took a deep breath.

"I'm Fuzzle," I informed her, hoping that she would share her name with me. She did.

"I'm Fransie," she said and dropped her gaze.

She was such a pretty little thing. I suddenly felt that I wanted to protect and care for her.

"Have you eaten?"

"A little," she said and her voice sounded embarrassed and apologetic. "I'm afraid that I'm not too good at hunting on my own yet."

"Well, come with me." I sounded a bit boastful. "I know just the spot."

I led her to the picnic area, and she squealed with delight when she found all of the good things. She ate daintily, but she sure was hungry.

After she had finished I took her to the pond. I wanted to shout to all of my friends and draw their attention to her, but I wasn't sure that it was the right thing to do.

After she had had all that she wanted to eat and drink, she turned to me.

"Thank you so much," she said. "You have been most kind. I appreciate it so much. Now I mustn't keep you any longer. If you're sure, really sure, that I won't be taking some of your territory, I'd like to stay in the area. If I will be a bother, then you must say so . . . please."

"No. No bother . . . really . . ." I stammered.

She smiled. "Then I must go and see if I can find a home before the sun—"

"But I was hoping," I cut in, "that is . . . well you see . . . I've been the only skunk in the area . . . and I've been lonely . . . really lonely . . . and, well . . . I was just so glad to see another one of my kind . . . and I was sorta hoping that . . . well . . . that we could be family —I mean . . . if you wouldn't mind. I know all of the area now—where to find water, where to find food. And I've already got a home—a great home—all dry and snug and even lined with feathers and . . ."

I stopped for breath. She was smiling again. Boy, she was pretty when she smiled.

"You're sure?" she said hesitantly.

"Yeah, I'm sure. I mean I'm really sure. Why, I thought that I might need to leave all of this—these woods, the pond, the picnic area, my home, everything—just to find family. Please . . ."

"That would be nice. I miss having a family." She smiled again, and I thought that I saw tiny tears in her eyes.

"Then it's settled," I said very matter-of-fact-like. Then I let some of my pent-up feelings come to the fore.

"Jiminy Whiz," I almost shouted. "Jiminy Whiz!"

I led the way home, my chest fairly swelled with pride and happiness. I wouldn't need to move away after all. I could share all of the good things of Pleasant Woods with Fransie.

As we moved toward our home, the morning sun was already peeking above the horizon; but it wasn't nearly as bright as my smile.